ENJOY!

Harjo

Janette

Informed
Connections
Installment 3
By Janette Harjo

Dedication

The names are too many to list, but I
would like to dedicate this - the third
story in my first published series - to
all those who have helped me with this as
teachers and readers, those who critiqued,
and those who motivated. Especially to my
sister Judy Crowe who beta read for me, my
mother, Annie Mae Simon who inspires me,
and to Romance Writers of America for
enabling me to have met all those who have
assisted in my journey to publication.

Chapter One

Present Day ~

 "Do you believe in magic?"

Valerie's mind echoed with the medieval magus' mysterious question. It tickled her inner femininity with the great medieval magician's erotic caress. She yearned for her dream lover's embrace before she opened her eyes to the new day.

She flexed and reached her arms out to her side, but her stomach tightened when her fingers found no one lay beside her. They recoiled from the vast vacancy of the cold cotton bed sheets at her side.

Her eyelids fluttered open to the reality of life as she knew it. The bright flowered wallpaper and white ceiling of her contemporary 21st century bedroom slowly came into focus. A knot grew in her stomach. *I can't be here. He can't be gone.*

She possessed a fervent desire to grasp her dream. In denial, Valerie once more swept her bare arm out across the bed beside her. Same as before, the furnishing disappointed her with its emptiness. She squeezed her eyes tight against a lonely tear, which escaped anyway.

Her body ached with barrenness at what seemed to her a timeless search for the man of her intended destiny. A fist of eternal emptiness clutched her gut. As always, there would be no peace to continue into another day.

Valerie rolled toward the middle of her double-wide bed and curled into the fetal position. She knew the day awaited, but couldn't force herself to throw the covers back and climb out of bed. She jerked wide-eyed when a passing bus' horn bellowed, but remained covered.

After a moment's meditation over whether or not she should get up; Valerie straightened and yanked the blankets further over her head in a frustrated fit of resignation. The darkness resumed her solitary retreat with a blanket's sigh.

She mulled her situation over in silence. Her eyelids twitched to open, but she didn't allow them to. *Why do I constantly dream about that man? It's like I know, or should know him. He's so real and familiar to me.*

Visions of the men Valerie knew appeared before her mind's eye. She couldn't conjure up a soul who matched the man in her dreams. *He'd be perfect for me.* She sucked her breath in. *Could this image in my dreams be an impression of the man I'm meant to love?*

Sudden motivation enabled her to leave her bed. *I've got to find this man.* She chuckled at herself in mid-motion. *He couldn't be real. I just have an amazing*

imagination. She shrugged her shoulders.
Oh, well; won't hurt if I look.

Her steps didn't still until she left
her bedroom behind her. *Even if he does
exist; I don't know where to look for him.
I don't know anyone like him. Will I ever
be fortunate enough to find this man who
will make my dreams come true?*

Internal commotion tormented her. *If
I haven't found him in my waking life, why
is this same man always with me in my
dreams?* Why did she always wake with such
a vast emptiness and longing for his
touch?

Valerie closed her eyes and placed
fingertips to her temples. Bright spots
of light danced inside her eyelids. She
held her head and stumbled to her bathroom
medicine chest for pain reliever.

She swallowed a couple of pills and
returned to her room. The sadness of the
moment encircled her like a shadowed veil,
and slipped her back under the bedcovers.
Valerie prayed the medicine would also ease
the pain her heart experienced.

Back in bed, she fought to hold onto
the visualization of her night's desires,
but it teased from the edge of her
recollection. She squeezed her eyelids
and did her very best to remember every
aspect of her dreams. *If I only believe
hard enough I might make them all come
true.*

Valerie inhaled, threw her covers
back, and bolted upright, but he failed to
materialize. Her wide-eyed hope he'd
reveal himself in front of her, failed
her. She laughed at herself, glad no one
could see what she just did.

At the realization of the idiocy she just hoped to accomplish, Valerie clasped her hands to the sides of her head and shook it in frustration. *This is just plain crazy. I've got to stop doing this to myself.*

Valerie stopped in mid-thought and compared her experiences to what she knew about schizophrenia. *Do I need to see a 'shrink'?* Her thought stabbed her heart; in her mind's eye she truly did see the magician as a real person.

The young volunteer social worker desired to leave the mundane reality of her lonely life behind. She wanted to remain with the man in her dreams, in the magic of his medieval world.

She stared into the full-length mirror on the door opposite her bed, and asked the young hazel-eyed woman with fiery brunette hair who faced her, "Am I going insane?" Valerie closed her eyes and flopped back onto her bed.

Later that morning, at the inner-city bus terminal, Valerie wrestled her fingers in her wallet to get her bus pass out. The business bustled with rushed commuters and busy buses while she waited for her own.

The morning citizenry surrounded and tormented her empathic spirit. What seemed more than its share of her laid-back city's less fortunate teemed through the bus-hub's boundaries. Hands held out to her at regular intervals.

"I need bus fare."

"Some money for a meal, ma'am?"

"Pardon me, ma'am. Could you help me out with some gas money?"

Valerie creased her eyebrows. It dissatisfied her she couldn't help all the city's destitute people. Some days the trials and tribulations of the crowds beset her worse than others. *I wish I could help you all, but I can't.*

Chapter Two

On days like today, Valerie especially wished she existed in the magical medieval dream world with her magnificent magician. The lover in her nighttime fantasies satisfied her in new ways every night.

Valerie snapped out of her subconscious and back to reality. She had a bus to catch and a day job to get to. *Get over it, Valerie. This is so silly of you. Dreams are dreams. Fantasies, that's all they are.*

She shook her head to clear it of her flights of fancy and focused on the reality of this day with all its worries. Her heart pounded amidst all the day's troubles while she returned to the search for her elusive bus pass.

A child's cry rose above the tumult around her. Valerie's fingers froze in mid-scramble. Her heart caught and she shifted her attention toward the sound. The child's voice sounded familiar. She looked around and listened.

It saddened her she couldn't discern

the cry's source. Her compassionate care-
giver's senses told her she'd heard more
of a whimper than an actual cry. No one
appeared in distress, but no doubt existed
in her mind she heard it.

The throng who hustled past her to
make their bus connections obliterated any
chance of her quick location of the lost
child. She fought to remain alert in the
inexplicable multitude of city travelers
crowded about her.

A harried mother with child in tow
cut in front of her. A long-haired bearded
man bumped into her during his frenzied
dash for a bus connection. Valerie
fumbled not to drop the small purse she
carried.

The terminal's constant commotion
disquieted her in a new way today. While
she'd lived here in this northwest
American city, so much activity never
before existed at this terminal. She
puzzled over its possible significance.

Valerie delved deep inside herself in
an attempt at isolation from the
distraught dispositions in the air.
Distance from the emotional strain enabled
her continued search for the bus pass in
the midst of all the craziness around her.

The remembered cry wouldn't leave
her. *That child needs my help.* She closed
her diminutive purse with a resigned sigh
and devoted her attention to a search for
him.

Frustration tightened her jaw when
the reason why she couldn't take time to
find the child right now came back to her.
Any other day she could have set her own
hours, but not today. *You have a court*

date, Valerie Baldwin.

She reopened her small wallet and resumed her exploration, but the distressed sound echoed in her mind. Valerie shaded her eyes from the morning sunlight with a hand, did another quick perusal of her surroundings, and forced herself back to the search for her bus pass.

"Do you believe in magic?"

Valerie's heart skipped when she heard the words she remembered so well from her morning's dream. She held her breath, froze, and widened her eyes all in the same instant. Tiny pinpricks of hope scurried through her chest.

Her recently discovered bus pass slipped from her fingers and her wallet metamorphosed back into a tiny hand-held purse - the bus permit tucked inside. She clamped her hands onto her little bag and raised it up so it rested under her chin.

Anticipatory adrenaline rushed up the center of Valerie's chest. Her heart fluttered as she turned toward the familiar voice. *My dream has come true?* She couldn't help but hope she'd meet the man from her dreams within the next minute.

Her peripheral vision caught a movement from the speaker. It directed her attention back to her wallet. She then realized her pass peeked out for her to grab again. The permit curled toward her in a sudden breeze, as if it said, "Here I am."

Valerie finished her turn toward the man who spoke. Her breath once more vanished at the vision before her eyes. She couldn't have run away even if she wanted to. Her knees softened and her heart raced.

Any thoughts of reality blanked from Valerie's mind. Her heart stilled. *He is the magician from my dreams. Has he finally come to save me from this loveless lifetime I exist in? Oh, please let it be true.*

The gold laced material of her new acquaintance's black suit matched that of the sorcerer's cloak she knew so well. A breeze tossed his trench-coat jacket's tail about his long lean legs. Golden brown chest hair peeked through his opened collar.

Valerie's professional rationale argued with her. *People don't walk out of dreams and into reality. He might be a man like the one I seek, or he might be a homeless soul with a line. Either way; he can't be the same magician I dream about.*

As Valerie inched her vision from his chest to his face, she wrestled with belief in her dream come true. Her gaze appreciated its crawl up the familiar view of his well-toned body, until it finally rested upon his face.

With his full facade in view, thousands of tiny cells collided in her head, as if from a caffeine fit. She dizzied and imagined herself lighter than air as she absorbed everything about his all too recognizable appearance.

Her vision of him entranced her. Only in her dreams had she seen those molten brown eyes before. He appeared as though he recognized her, too. *I can't believe this is happening to me.*

Chapter Three

Unanticipated expectations raced through Valerie at her dream lover's sudden appearance. A sudden breeze chilled the moisture on her forehead. She shivered from the heat.

The man's eyes appeared as though their vision traveled past her heated reaction. It seemed they saw through to her very soul. Only their implied trespass on her consciousness prevented her emotional dive into any comfort their warmth offered.

His appearance invoked erotic memories from her dreams into her thoughts. They added to her moment's torture. Valerie lowered her gaze in an instant of self-consciousness. She struggled to remain calm, but couldn't control her blood's pulse.

Her facial moisture refused to evaporate. What if her fantasies were proven wrong and the man from her dreams didn't really stand there with her.

The man's mischievous brown eyes mystified her from between luscious dark

lashes she envied so much. She estimated
he stood at least half a foot over her own
height of 5'5". *The same as in my dreams.*
His proximity sent her senses into
craziness.

His dark brown hair shone almost
black, but not quite. Its ends toyed with
the top of his coat's collar. Highlights
of starlit splendor in his hair flashed in
the day's sunlight. It continually changed
its hues before her enraptured eyes.

Over-excitement tingled through
Valerie's core and beyond. She ached to
pursue the rebirth of her nightly
emotional urges, but his implied authority
commanded her obeisance, just as it did
while she slept.

Valerie remained in suspended
animation while her admiration continued.
She appreciated anew the strength in the
man's eyebrows. They matched in color his
chest hair, which toyed with her senses
from above his clothing.

His brown eyes, impish though they
may be, sparkled out to her in their
familiar way. They titillated her to the
very deepest essence of her soul. She
recalled how they, along with the rest of
his mannerisms, inspired her to throes of
ecstasy each night.

His proportionate straight nose led
her vision down to a set of full, sensual
lips. They seductively blended into his
strong chin. Intense memory of how those
lips aroused her, in the most intimate
ways during his nighttime kisses,
stimulated her almost to the point of
improper behavior.

Her fingers quivered with memory.

14

They ached to reach out - to touch him. She longed to let them play in the hair on his head. They wanted to trail down his chest to the curls that covered it and further downward still.

Just as she felt her face begin its warmth into a telltale shade of red with her overly intimate thoughts, Valerie gripped reality and averted her vision. She mentally slapped herself for staring at the poor unsuspecting stranger like a child at a candy store.

When she glanced back and their eyes caught, it seemed as if the two of them became inseparable. The rest of the world ceased to exist for Valerie. *It's as if he has cast a spell on me.* Her heart quivered. *Perhaps my dream has come true.*

It appeared to her the unknown, yet familiar man stiffened in revulsion the moment his eyes met with hers. *Why'd he do that?* He broke contact with her and visually searched around the transit center. It appeared as if he searched for something, but couldn't be sure of what.

Valerie experienced a pain at that moment, such as she'd never known before. An uneasy current she could only associate with déjà vu beset her. It speared through her like a stake of guilt that burnt until she could bear it no more. Did he experience the pain, too?

The torture needed to be stopped. It no longer mattered if he wanted nothing more to do with her. She too found she wanted nothing to do with this man whose presence caused her so much pain, which seemed so familiar.

When he once more accepted her

15

glance; something poignant in his shadowed
eyes told her he indeed endured the same
agony she did. *We will only cause each
other pain.*

Her heart caved-in with the stark
revelation. Where'd her sudden knowledge
come from? *What don't I remember?* Her
consciousness lightened from lack of
oxygen.

The man in front of her shivered. It
appeared to be involuntary, as if he shook
the same sensation as her away from
himself. Valerie suffered her own
reflexive shiver.

She couldn't face any more of it,
just as it appeared he wouldn't face his.
She broke her empathic connection with
him. *I can't allow the union of our like
knowledge.*

The stranger's hand went to his chin
where it massaged, as if he deliberated on
the matter she dismissed. Then it
appeared he accepted the breakage of their
connection when he set his gaze a fraction
askance from hers.

The stammer he ensued with came in a
way that seemed very odd to come from a
man who appeared so full of self-control
and assurance, "I-I'm sorry. Please
forgive me. I took you for someone else."

His clipped words came to her as he
turned and began a quick pace away. With a
whoosh, his stylish black trench coat swept
after him in the billows created by his
swift departure.

"Forgive me," he reiterated as he
left. Valerie's vague knowledge of her
long ago hurt, and imagination of how he
once suffered because of her, twisted her

stomach as she watched him leave. She stared after him when he vacated her company as abruptly as he appeared.

She quivered with the anxiety she endured. *It all seems so real. It's too real.* She rolled her head back and lifted her gaze to the heavens. *How do I know what I do?*

In spite of her like emotions, her memory of his hardened expression of total repugnance plagued her. Valerie's emotions called out to him. The twist in her gut rose to her heart and into her throat.

He looked like the lover I've dreamt about for so many years. How could he just leave me here? His definitive action left her at a loss for reason.

Chapter Four

Valerie's face fell slack at his retreat. As her stomach knotted, she clutched it and massaged. The pain distressed her insides in a way she knew, but couldn't bring to her mind.

Her knees resumed their softened stance. In her instance of misery she shuffled to an unoccupied passenger bench and sat. Her forehead slapped into her palms as a myriad of questions pummeled her brain.

My perception has struck me with so much more force this time than ever before. What did I just see? How'd I see it? I only see into troubled children, not myself or other adults.

She didn't have the time or the energy to take on any new problems. Valerie reiterated to herself she only saw into the minds of the children who needed her help. *And that is the way it must remain.*

Valerie refocused her thoughts on the day's little abused client. *She'll be at the courthouse waiting for me this morning.* It'd taken Valerie and her co-workers a long year of hard work to get the case to where it now stood.

As the child's court appointed temporary advocate/guardian, Valerie needed to see the judge put her small charge in a safe place. *I will pay attention to my dreams on my own time; not on little Katie's time.*

In spite of her new determination, Valerie's success in diverting her mind to business enjoyed a short-lived life. Her glimpse of the stranger's past trauma worked its way back into her thoughts like a nightmare her subconscious already knew.

Her recent experience challenged her to distraction. No matter how hard she tried, Valerie couldn't hold her concentration back from her morning's acquaintance and place it on the day's events. They'd soon be upon her and would need her full attention when they arrived.

Not until auto-pilot overtook Valerie, would force of habit propel her on into her day's planned activities. She stared down the street and hoped against hope to see her bus on its way into the terminal.

I must keep this morning's brief acquaintance off my mind. She breathed a sigh of relief when, at long last, the bulky vehicle she awaited lumbered around the corner. Its well-used brakes ground in announcement of its arrival.

Finally. Valerie's heart calmed at the appreciated sight of her expected sanctuary. The gray with yellow trim bus neatly pulled into an empty space between the other filling buses, and parked.

Its familiar whine of released gears, along with the warm current of motor-oil scented air, cleared Valerie's mind of her dream lover and forced reality back onto her. The vehicle's time-worn door folded open and she ascended onboard the bus' foot scarred steps.

Without even a thought about it, she glanced back out into the terminal area through the driver's side window as she climbed into the vehicle. Her vision immediately caught on the same man who spoke to her earlier. The sight of him reawakened all her secret fantasies.

He posed in confidence on the curb, as if he waited for her to return his attention. The figure he struck imposed on her as he stood balanced with his legs spread apart in a vee pose she seemed to remember from somewhere in her past.

The stranger held his arms crossed over his chest. He appeared to be the master of all he surveyed. His hypnotic smile sent thrills of pleasure through her most sensitive areas. Her heart fluttered and she gasped in silence.

He's back. *Did he ever leave?* She touched her hair. *Is he looking at me?* Her fingers twirled in the long waves of her wind-swept hairstyle.

Within moments, Valerie re-emerged from the world where only the two of them existed, and noticed others occupied the terminal area along with him. The transferring passengers milled about him while they boarded their buses.

A twinge of jealousy twisted in her heart whenever a young woman glanced his way with a sweet smile as she passed by with a swing of her hips. But it appeared he ignored the other women at the bus center. His eyes seemed only for Valerie.

Recognition of his gaze eased her unwarranted anxiety at the obvious flirtations of the other ladies present. His suggestive expression tantalized her with erotic warmth. It spread through her and melted her insides.

Valerie's blood buzzed with an excited pulse through her. *He's interested in me after all.* On that exhilarated thought she again took her attention away from him, and returned it into the vehicle.

Her initial gaze landed on the bus-driver. The gray-haired and potbellied man drained the last of his drink from his cup and plopped it back onto its thermos. By his beverage's aromatic smell, Valerie assumed it to be coffee.

He wiped his mouth with the back of his gray-brown hair-tufted hand and smiled through his coffee stained teeth at her.

"Good morning, Valerie!"

She smiled and returned his amiable greeting, "Hi, Joe. How are ya?"   She recalled how the friendly driver had driven this route for all the nine years she'd traveled on it. Through all their time spent riding together, they'd become dear friends.

Out of habit, even though she knew the driver didn't require he see it, she flashed her worn bus pass. In the same movement; she then began her customary trek down the long scuffed aisle of the aged bus he drove.

Chapter Five

The familiar people in the bus smiled back at Valerie while she squeezed her way through in search of a seat. Unfamiliar passengers diverted their vision from hers or ignored her as if she didn't even exist.

She held her breath at the stagnant atmosphere of the close quarters. The fall day's unusual warmth increased with each step she took. Body heat inside the vehicle clashed with the combined aromas of various perfumes.

Valerie wrinkled her nose as she passed through the odor-laden air. Discolored faces greeted her passage. She pitied them. For all she knew they might also be allergic to the mass of perfumed sprays. She thanked her God she had no allergies.

But the heavens knew she needed to breathe. She swept her vision around her perimeters and searched for what she perceived would be a miracle - a seat beside an opened window where she could take in some fresh air.

She inadvertently bumped into a few

of the riders as she threaded her way down the narrow aisle in search of an available seat. Most took up a part of the aisle alongside their seat with either body or paraphernalia overhang.

Valerie smiled appreciatively when she finally spied a free seat. Her find became more prized when she noticed it also happened to be a window seat. *Praise God! This will make today's bus ride much more enjoyable.*

She stepped in from the aisle to the seat. A small passenger dressed in tattered clothes sat next to the aisle. Once in, and before she sat, Valerie dragged the window down its rusted frame. It screeched and jerked against her insistence.

On a mission; Valerie struggled against the oxidized mechanics until she obtained her objective. After she accomplished her mission; she stuck her nose out and inhaled a deep breath of fresh air before she sat.

When she did so, a gushy sound filled the air and she discovered why the window seat remained vacant on the packed to its limit bus. Her face flamed as whatever she sat in bubbled from the bench-seat.

Valerie immediately wished her attention hadn't centered on the window before she sat. The air bubbled and fizzled and popped under her. Something greasy oozed through the slacks of her new navy blue suit onto her bare thighs underneath.

Everybody stared at her. A few of the younger passengers chuckled. Her face heated in humiliation under everyone's perusal. She remained seated and debated on what she should do next.

While she endeavored to discern the source of her embarrassment, Valerie lifted and twisted in observation of her seat. She hoped her actions convinced those around her the sound hadn't been what they obviously thought.

Valerie groaned at the site presented. Her stomach turned queasy at her sight of oily greenish and brownish goo on the seat. She sniffed in disgust and engaged in a sheepish peek around at her onlookers before her gaze returned to the seat.

The little boy who sat in the place beside the suspect spot sunk back in his seat as if it sucked him in. He giggled in hysterics and snorted through the hand he covered his face with. Tears streamed down his cheeks.

The young volunteer social worker thought him cute, in spite of himself. He looked up at her through his thick blond lashes, and snickered, "That was funny! I tricked ya, huh? I know lots of tricks!"

Even though he laughed at her, Valerie couldn't take insult at his animated merriment. Something in his voice gripped her, but she let it go.

She looked at the greasy substance all over the boy's hands and saw a shiny molding wrapper on his lap; it read, "Bubble-Goop! The Messiest Stuff In The World!"
She gave her expression a sarcastic twist and thought of the like sarcasm in its logo, *"Parents the 'World' over love it!"*

The package's unappreciated words of

irony sunk in Valerie's chest as she looked down to her initial choice for a bus seat once more. In resignation, she sat in the mess again. *My clothes are already ruined for today, anyway.*

Her predicament continued to turn her stomach as the young culprit squeezed more of the melted goop between his fingers. It oozed between them like moist, warm excrement. The sight brought her last meal to her throat.

A small groan of self-sympathy escaped her at the thought of her need for fresh clothes. *One more thing I don't need today.* She entertained a quick last minute change of plans and tensed to regain her feet.

But the floor's vibration under her, as Joe idled the bus, stayed her impulse. Even though she lived in a nearby condo, Valerie considered the plan B she initially pictured wasn't an option.

She couldn't just run home and change. *I can't expect the bus to wait for me.* The oils the boy's doughy diversion contained probably meant the ruin of her new silk suit, regardless of what the advertisements claimed about the substance's easy clean attributes.

She'd need to go shopping for new clothes before her day began. Valerie's only alternative necessitated a stop at a mall they'd pass by on their way to her stop. *Plan C. It would never do for me to show up in court looking like this.*

Valerie glanced at the time on her phone and frowned at how fast the day sped by. That didn't change the new plans forced upon her. Knowledge of the mess

made it easier for Valerie to deal with
what she needed to do.

She glared at the hysterical little
boy in mock anger.

The child stilled at her question and
stared at her. All his previous bravado
vanished. His eyes revealed a depth of
hurt Valerie knew she hadn't inflicted on
him.

He sniffled and ran his tattered
sleeve across his runny nose. "My Ma? She
don' care."

Chapter Six

Valerie's throat lumped. Her concern
as a child advocate emerged. "Where is
your mother?" she softly murmured. She
shifted toward him, clasped his sticky
hands into hers, and gave them a soft
massage.

Love flowed from her to him through
Valerie's tender hands. She closed her
eyes. Her depth of emotion for this child
equaled what she experienced at the bus
station. She strengthened her resolve and
attempted connection with him.

The boy jerked his hands from hers.
"I don' know," he stated. His tattered
sleeve slid up his arm when he wiped his
runny nose on it again. His movement
betrayed a nasty bruise.

Valerie held her breath with a sharp
intake of air. Her heart ached for him.
Memories of like-wounds on a childhood
friend flooded her mind's eye. The
unpleasant purple color struck a horror
into her she'd never forget.

She closed her eyes and called on her
moral values for self-composure before

total loss of control claimed her. Her new state of mind enabled her professional examination of the sight before her. *That is the mark of a vicious grip.*

The large lump reformed in her throat and empathy claimed her. Unshed tears glands filled her eyes. *Who has done this to this poor child?* She delved into the boy's mind and searched for answers, but found none. *He's closed himself off.*

Pictures of the bruises she'd seen of that type before now instead filled her mind. Sally, her childhood friend, wore them before the girl's unfortunate death by parental abuse at the tender age of five.

Valerie stiffened and fought the distraction of her repressed memory.

I can't break down now. She trembled and struggled to keep her tenuous grip on calm. *I must ignore my eternal rage.*

Anger always roared within her when her unwelcome childhood memory bared its ugly head, as it did so often in her work with unwanted children. She changed the subject with her seat partner, "Are you on your way to school?"

"No."

"No? Why not?"

"I don' go to school."

"Why not?" she repeated.

He held up all five fingers on one of his hands and squealed at her, "Because I don' need to go!" His wide-eyed expression of innocence told her he thought her an idiot, "I'm only five years old!"

The dreadful ache from before wrenched Valerie's heart and choked her with tears. *Sally's age.* Once more she pushed the dreadful memory away and directed her attention onto her newest project.

"You're big for your age, aren't you?" The skinny young man's long legs belied his stated age.

"'taint none of your business," the boy snapped, as if in an act of defense he knew too well.   He jumped up and ran off the still parked bus before Valerie found a response.

She froze with an index finger raised toward him. It amazed her at how expertly he threaded his way between the harried passengers who still boarded the bus. *He's accomplished at escape.*

She imagined she'd witnessed a lone tear in his eye as the boy ran away from her. She thawed and started to her feet as she found her voice. "Hey! Wait!" she called in mid-rise from her seat.

The boy didn't even pause long enough to look back at the sound of her voice. Valerie panicked at her loss of him. In pursuit, she forced her way among the riders already on the vehicle, and through the new passengers who boarded.

By the time she reached the bus' opened door, the child she chased disappeared into the crowd. Many milled about in the terminal area. Behind her, the bus driver called for her attention and she turned back to him with a frown on her face.

Joe rested his amiable gaze on her and asked, "Will I be losing the pleasure of your company so soon?"

Valerie smiled her thanks for and acceptance of the driver's implied regret at her departure. She imagined how her mad dash to the front of the bus must have left her appearance disheveled, and brushed a wayward lock of her long layered brunette hair from her forehead.

With no time for words, she redirected her focus back outside and resumed her visual search of the busy area. It frustrated her she couldn't see the whole of the station's grounds from inside the door of the bus.

Whether consciously or not, Valerie also scanned the area for her recent acquaintance. But when she recognized her uncalled for hunt, she put aside any fantasies she might still harbor about him and returned to her call in life.

She answered the bus driver's question as she corrected her wayward purpose, "No, not leaving the bus. I'm looking for that little boy who just scooted off here. Did you see which way he went?" she asked over her shoulder.

Joe's initial reply amounted to not much more than a grunt. Valerie wondered at it as she eagerly continued her visual hunt out through the bus' warped and cracked folded open door.

The driver's next comment troubled her. She thought him more compassionate. But he didn't sound like he much cared about what happened to the boy.

"Didn't pay for his bus fare. Just as well he's gone. I can't keep paying for him. I've seen 'im just hanging around this terminal a lot of times before.

"It's kind of like he lives here or somewhere around here, anyways." Joe's tone changed to one of what sounded like the concern Valerie expected from him as he continued, "Poor kid. Probably a run away."

Valerie's inner alarm peaked at the driver's contemplative words. She gave her head a slow compassionate shake, which matched Joe's tone, and continued with her thoughts about the boy, "You say he's here a lot?

"I've never noticed him around here before. Has anybody ever reported the boy's constant loitering, or the implied homelessness of his situation?" Her heart renewed its anxious race with the degree of her wonderment.

Joe nodded his late middle-aged head. "Oh yeah, sure. It's been reported. Whenever the authorities have come around and looked for him, he can't be found. The kid just kind of disappears. It's like magic."

Like magic? A chill ran up her chest. Valerie chased away recollection of her day's first acquaintance and continued her visual search with the diligence of her profession. She sighed when she found no sign of the boy.

Valerie's heart thrummed with her concern. Sure enough, he'd just "disappeared," like Joe told her. She held her forehead in her hands and massaged her worry-ravaged temples with her thumbs. *What will become of that poor child?*

Valerie knew she needed to find a way to determine the boy's identity and establish connection with him. A lump formed in her throat at the imagined consequences of his forlorn situation, if she didn't find and help him.

She searched deep inside herself in a

desperate need to see more about the boy, but couldn't sufficiently clear her mind of the man whom she just met. *Why do the man and the boy seem so intertwined? Why are they both in my life right now?*

Second considerations about if she should've pursued conversation with her earlier acquaintance plagued her. They clouded her ability to perceive anything about the boy or his plight.

Chapter Seven

Valerie's memory of her earlier acquaintance filled the compassionate social worker with concern she couldn't ignore. She accepted she needed to take the gamble of her earlier acknowledgment and know more about him, before she could forget and move on.

The man's past trauma cried out to her. Maybe if he hadn't left her so abruptly, there might have been something she could've done to help him. *Could whatever happened in his past be the reason I dream about him?* Her heart muscles twisted.

Valerie stared into space, lost in her thoughts and oblivious to the new riders who shoved past her. The connectedness she experienced with the magician stole her breath. *It's the same as I have with children.*

Memory of when her eyes first opened to her gift for mental communication with youngsters returned. She flooded with new compassion and couldn't swallow when the all too familiar tightness returned to her throat.

Poor Sally. Her childhood friend's parents hadn't paid, but from her youth Valerie vowed she'd see justice done. *If not for Sally, then for another child.* Her job throughout her adult life enabled her to see fair deals done for many other children.

Her remembrance of the good she did enabled Valerie's mind-switch to today's court appearance. She knew she'd see justice done once more. Her purpose today would be the completion of taking a child, like Sally, away from her abusive parents.

Valerie relished the good sentiments that came from righting what few wrongs in the world she could. She wished she could do more. *If only magic really did exist. A magic that would protect all the little children would be a perfect magic.*

Her deliberations on magic brought on fantasies about the man of her most recent encounter. Could he have really been the man from her dreams? *Stop it, Valerie! You have a child to protect.*

Her self-endowed righteousness returned with the sizzle of her profession. *If only I could be left alone with the parents who abused the child I'll see in court today.*

Valerie's first choice would be the ability to reason with such parents. She'd change them and make them better people, not take their children away. But history had shown, people such as she dealt with didn't respond to reason.

Parents such as that don't see their children as individual human beings. She swallowed down the reality they only saw their children as possessions that could be abused and tossed. That fact always presented itself as a bitter truth for her.

Valerie raised her face heavenward and closed her moist eyes in a moment of prayerful meditation. Reflections and counseling would be her initial therapy with the boy from the bus terminal, if she ever came into contact with him again.

"Valerie?"

She jerked back to attention when Joe's rusty voice worked its way back into her conscious thoughts.

Before she had an opportunity to respond to her friend, a young man who lugged a large frayed psychedelic colored canvas bag clambered onto the bus and bumped it into her as he passed.

Valerie lost her balance, but regained it with a quick ball change of her feet.

"Oh! I forgot where I was," She acknowledged to the driver. Valerie accepted she stood in the way of the other passengers who wanted to ride the same bus as her, so she stepped aside and excused herself to everyone.

In her search for a place to hide while she shared words with Joe, she slipped into a little niche between the bus' steering column and console. It offered her convenience, even though she knew it only offered refuge until the bus moved on.

Valerie inhaled, and made herself as small as possible. It gratified her; others now passed by with no effort. She focused on old Joe and devoted her full attention to his line of conversation, which remained on their earlier topic.

"A kid his age oughta be in school this time a day," he grumbled.

Valerie considered he sounded much like a father would. "That 'kid' told me he's too young to be in school."

"Hogwash," Joe spat out. "The boy's gotta be at least six or seven years old. First or second grade, anyway."

"He told me he was only five," Valerie uttered in soft retrospect as she again looked out the door after the child. She wondered at herself for her quick belief in what the boy told her.

"Probably just didn't want to get into too much trouble for his mischief. I'll guarantee you that he's being truant from school," Joe pronounced. By way of a change in subject he grimaced and offered her a dirty old towel from under the worn vinyl of his seat.

"Here, this might help you to clean up a bit," he muttered unhappily.

Valerie accepted the proffered rag from him, but paid no attention to its condition, or the purpose she'd use it for. Her focus stayed on the bus driver.

"I sure do hope I don't have to call for another bus," Joe grumbled. He rustled up another raggedy towel from the same place under his dirty gray plastic seat and followed his new passengers back to Valerie's vacated seat.

"The boy let on like his mother doesn't care about him. He said he doesn't even know where she is," Valerie worried to the driver's humped-over back as he shuffled his heavy shape away from

her and into the body of the claustrophobic
vehicle.

Chapter Eight

Valerie glanced back out the opened door in search of the boy, and for a breath of fresh air in an effort to realign her emotions.   The action brought her back to the immediacy of the moment.

In her tunnel-vision to find the boy, the issue of her soiled slacks slipped her mind until she remembered her acceptance of the old towel. Her face heated and her jawbone relaxed at her realization of what just happened.

Joe examined the seat of my pants. When she raised up her hand to her front and stared at the filthy rag it held, her moment of embarrassment turned to one of disbelief. The soil-encrusted old oil-stained towel left much to be desired.

"Hhhh." She imagined the seat of her pants would be grimier after she used the piece of tattered cloth on them, but reached behind herself and did so anyway. *Oh, well. It can't make them any worse.*

Valerie shook her head and grimaced in frustration when she glanced at her watch again. It showed late morning to her. Court began in an hour, and it'd take the bus she rode on a good ten or fifteen minutes to reach the shopping center.

Her mind whirled her options around in it like popcorn in a hot-air popper, but she knew there'd be no other way around her need for new clothes. *My shopping will just have to be done at a run. Good thing the court house isn't far away.*

She glanced back out the door after the boy and mentally chastised his worthless mother for his, hers, and everyone's predicament this morning. A spidery sensation wiggled through her when she again saw the stranger who earlier questioned her about magic, instead of relief at sight of the child she sought.

The man still stood in his original position, like he'd never left at all. He still wore the smile he'd mesmerized her with before. She couldn't help but physically respond to the come-hither expression he sent her.

Joe returned, harried from his unexpected janitorial mission, and resumed his speech. It seemed he responded to her thoughts about the boy's mother, "Yes, Ma'am. It's a shame some people don' watch after their kids any better."

He huffed. "They put 'em on here with me, and I'm their babysitter. There oughta be a law preventing some people from being parents."

Valerie jerked her head back to complete attention at the sound of his voice. She wondered if she'd somehow transmitted her thought patterns about the boy, to the driver. She chose not to worry about it though, and nodded in agreement.

She then turned her backside away from Joe, toward the metal divider between him and his passengers, and rubbed viciously on the seat of her pants. The material stuck to her upper thighs and bottom as she wiped it.

A quick twist of her waist for examination showed her the dirty rag did nothing noticeable for her slacks. She sighed and continued her attempt to do the best job she could with the grimy towel, anyway.

A few unruly half-grown kids in the back of the bus laughed and pointed at her.

Valerie ignored them and worked at the impossible solution to remedy her soiled situation.

Joe hollered back and shook his fist at the rudeness behind him. "You boys mind your manners!"

They quieted only enough to demonstrate they'd heard him. A few snickers followed.

A motherly, middle-aged woman seated in the front seat dug through her well-worn canvas book-bag sized handbag. "Oh dear; what a pity. Old Joe shouldn't have expected you'd be able to clean the mess up with that dirty ol' rag," she mumbled. "Here, I should have something cleaner in my purse you can use."

Even though Valerie's attention focused on her job, she experienced sincere appreciation for the woman's timely offer. She allowed herself a quick peek up and became inwardly amused at her benefactor.

The portly late middle-aged woman

made a comical show as she rummaged through her oversized piece of personal luggage. She tossed stuff to each of her sides and onto the laps of her seat-mates.

She pulled out a couple of well-read paperback books, a few small grandchild type toys, and a worn plastic leather wallet before she paused as if in wonder of where her wipes could be. Within the next minute, her renewed search revealed a ring of what appeared to be house and car keys.

A few other miscellaneous odds and ends followed. Her most recent finds included a deck of cards, a few plastic tubes of lotion, and some bottles. No ink remained on the used bottles to show their brand or their prescribed use.

The woman who showed her timely support for Valerie finally found the object for which she dug. "Here, I found it." She stared at her bag. "I knew I had this somewhere in here. It's only an almost used up old package of hand tissues, but here you go."

She wrinkled her nose and squeezed her eyes so she looked at Valerie through a slit between her lids for a moment. "They're a bit unsightly, but at least they're clean."

Valerie, whose mission with her handheld towel on her pants never ceased for an instant while the woman searched, finally took a break from the task. She straightened and acknowledged the woman's assistance with a smile.

She belatedly recognized the friendly passenger as a seat partner of hers from times passed. "Thank you, Mrs. Applegate. I'm sorry, but I've been so involved here I didn't recognize you or the sound of your voice."

Mrs. Applegate smiled. "Oh, don't you give it a worry, honey."

Valerie accepted the fresh, crumpled up wipes, and continued in her mission - for what difference it made.

Joe, who took in all the verbal exchange between the two of his passengers, asked Valerie, "Who was that young man in the all gussied up clothes I saw talking to you as I pulled my bus up to the station?"

Valerie returned his towel to him; tossed the wipes she used into the bus' small plastic waste basket and wrapped her arms around the bus driver in a big bear hug. She valued her friendship with Joe. He treated her like the father she never had.

She glanced back out the door and her femininity once more responded to the sight before her eyes. The stranger still stood in place, as if he waited for her to disembark and join him. His eyes continued their captivation of her.

The man, whom by now Valerie sensed was indeed a magician, lifted his left brow in response to her fascinated gaze. His mannerism plucked the strings of her attraction to him. She experienced what she likened to an eternal yearning.

"That's a good question," she quietly wondered aloud, more to herself than in answer to Joe.

Chapter Nine

Valerie sniffed and blinked her eyes. *I've never been so affected by any man. He seems to be quite aware of his charisma, which he no doubt uses to his advantage with women.* She shrugged. *I'll probably never see him again, anyway.*

She turned her head, forced her attention away from the man who beckoned it, and pulled her mind out of its recent erotic fantasies. *This isn't like me.*

"Thanks for cleaning my seat, Joe," she commented. Now she'd need to once more venture into the packed bus and reclaim the place she laid claim on.

"You're welcome," he replied. "I don't know if it's clean, but I did the best job I could for ya."

Valerie tried not to allow it, but the magician's captivating face etched itself into her thoughts after she resumed her position in the public vehicle. Her insatiable curiosity niggled at her without stop.

Does he still watch after me? She glanced aside and took what she hoped would be considered an inconspicuous peek out the window beside her. Her sly visual search expanded as far into the terminal as she could see.

When she didn't see the supposed man from her dreams anywhere, her heart sank. *He's gone.* She told herself it didn't matter. *He must have left in search of another as soon as I continued back into the bus.*

She sighed. *Well enough. Had I really hoped to see him there? Am I conceited enough to have thought that delicious man had nothing better to do than stand around all day looking after me?*

After her moment of self-chastisement, and against all her better impulses, Valerie took another peek through the downed side-window. She noticed the entire place had cleared of the passengers who previously milled around the terminal.

A shiver traced her skin when she recalled the larger than normal previous crowd. She strained her vision, but couldn't find a trace of the magician. He'd vanished, just like the little boy and everyone else.

Shock overwhelmed Valerie and she pressed back into the seat. A shiver of déjà vu sped through her when she remembered her brief acquaintance's two appearances... and disappearances. *Just like magic.*

Valerie remained in her seat as the vehicle rumbled under her and rolled out onto the city street. Her hands shook in time with her heart rate. *What's going on with me?*

Her brief acquaintance with the man at

the bus terminal wreaked havoc on her usual state of mental self-control. She scrunched her shoulders up to her ears and gave a tiny shake in order to regain that solid aspect of her nature.

She needed to be in full control of her senses to serve as a convincing witness in the courtroom today. But she couldn't refocus. Her curiosity remained on the man at the bus station. *Who could he have been and why did he affect me like he did?*

Valerie emerged from her daydream and trained her eyes on her unplanned shopping destination. It grew larger on the horizon each minute. She pulled on the old bus' frayed disembark cord. *BING*! The next bus stop sat in front of her new destination.

A glance at her wristwatch told her it hadn't taken as long to arrive at the shopping center as she'd imagined. She smiled in gratefulness. *The bus' early arrival gives me five extra minutes to shop.*

The vehicle pulled into the bus stop within minutes, but not quickly enough for Valerie. A zipper on her purse caught on the seat's frayed cloth when she jumped up from the well-worn place where she sat. She jerked it free and wobbled toward the front of the bus before it completed its stop.

Valerie reached the front and clung onto the stability bar at the door. She managed to keep her balance as Joe rolled his bus toward the space. She brightened while she stood in wait and planned use for every minute of the extra time available.

Joe arched his eyebrows as she stood at his side. Instead of his usual smile of greeting, he gave Valerie the "evil eye." She knew the reason behind it.

Valerie gave the driver an amiable smile. "I know. I know. I'm breaking the bus rules."

The driver didn't verbally chide her about her violation of his bus' policies, though. He just continued smooth brake pressure and slipped into the roadside space provided for him to park. He rolled his vehicle to a stop and cut the engine behind a couple other parked buses in the bus lane.

"Make haste! I'll only be here a short while." he commented as Valerie hopped off the bus and trotted toward the shopping establishment's entrance.

"Thanks!" she called back over her shoulder as she ran, not that he'd arrived there at the time he did expressly for her. She dodged a few cars as they moved throughout the lot. One horn sounded at her hurried zigzag through the busy area.

Out of breath before she reached the store she targeted, Valerie slowed in acquiescence of the upset driver. She didn't appreciate the car's driver made a spectacle of her in the lot. *Not that my crazy dash hasn't already done that.*

Chapter Ten

Valerie finished her shopping in short time and resumed her race for the courthouse. Back onboard the bus, deliberations about today's case filled her mind. She deemed the day she foresaw, in her haste to get it started, should be quite simple.

I probably didn't need to be so particular about the slacks I chose. The case nears its end. What she didn't expect was what today would really be all about.

Valerie's chest tightened and her step faltered outside the city's home of legal proceedings. The aged gothic styled building overshadowed her. She tensed in the menace of its unfamiliar aura.

Her intuitive inner vision tingled. Vague spidery fingers threaded through her psyche. The uninvited sensation threw her into a state of unusual loss. She focused on the world around her and called on her natural gift in an effort to understand.

She ran a slow gaze of its every facet

from end to end of the massive structure, before she took to the building. Chills traversed her shoulders, and déjà vu warped through her core when she entered the courthouse.

The door hinges groaned behind Valerie. She assumed their moan came after her entrance through the heavy mahogany doors, and paid it no mind. The ancient grizzled man who entered behind her, stared after her with the same menace as outside.

Inside, the business day progressed as would be expected for a busy city courthouse. Bailiffs ensured safe and secure courtrooms. A few men in dress slacks stood at a digital bulletin board and read the docket.

Valerie assumed they did so to determine when their cases would be heard. No smoke polluted the building's inside air.

Except for a few hushed conversations, quiet prevailed and no children could be seen or heard.

The normalcy calmed Valerie's nerves from her earlier moment of menace. She entered the temporary courthouse office of the volunteer-run Sunview Children's Services Organization in a much better mood.

The SCSO's main office existed in a church in downtown Sunview, Oregon. It occupied this court-house office only on a temporary basis when they had a child to place. It'd be a relief to Valerie when she saw today's situation through.

A new potential adoptive parent was

slated to appear for the court's
consideration today. She hoped it would
be a good fit between the adopter, whom she
didn't know, and the adoptee, who held a
special place in her heart.

Chapter Eleven

The child Valerie worked for sat quietly in SCSO's temporary office when she entered the room. One of her co-workers sat with the unfortunate at a short child-sized table. The little girl appeared totally absorbed in a picture she drew.

The four year old, dressed in Pinocchio pajamas, didn't at first notice Valerie's entrance into the room. The moment she gently closed the door behind her is when the girl acknowledged her presence and sprang from her seat. "Baleri!"

Valerie barely had time to drop to one knee in response to catch it as a little ball of blonde-haired energy bustled across the floor and into her opened arms. "Good Morning, Katie!" She scooped the curly headed child up and into her arms and carried her across the room to the desk where Katie's artwork rested.

"I go home wit'chu today?" the exuberant wide-eyed child entreated.

"I wish I could take you home with me today, honey, but I can't," Valerie murmured as she snuggled the girl to her. The little charge she held wilted like a neglected plant. Valerie remained as excited as she could, for the child's sake.

She held the little girl out in front of her and looked into the child's face. "But we're going to meet some people today who might be a new mommy and daddy for you!" She hugged Katie and sent her co-worker a hopeful glance.

Valerie worked with the mental and emotional needs of displaced children, while another department handled their placement. She didn't agree with the system at times, but she worked where children who needed her emphatic skills existed.

Valerie finished her day at the computer in SCSO's theater office with a young co-worker. When her eye caught a door's movement in the auditorium below them, she refocused on a man who entered with a strong-stride of self-confidence.

He wore a long black coat, and carried a gold tipped black cane artfully angled in his hands in front of him. Her heart arced at his implied majesty, and she remembered him as in a slow-motion before now moment.

Of course. She recognized him as the man she'd run into earlier. Valerie squinted her eyes in wonder at his appearance in SCSO's theater. Her breath caught at the assumption he could be the entertainment she'd hired. *Interesting.*

"Valerie? Earth to Valerie." Her new work-study student teased.

"Oh.   Excuse me," Valerie answered.

Her thought processes needed to be returned to the subject at hand, where she stood in the manager's booth at the theater. Her attention returned to her apt student worker.

She pulled her curious thoughts from the unexpected person in the auditorium, and refocused on her much younger assistant. They needed to continue their work on the computerized logistics for the approaching evening's entertainment.

Valerie tapped a few keys on the computer keyboard and pulled a new program up. "This is the way it works. Now you can go right in and it'll find whatever you ask it to."

"Thanks. I'm sure I can handle it now," her competent co-worker commented.

Valerie smiled and gave her teen-aged assistant a friendly pat on the back. The local high school work experience program had sent a very apt student to help coordinate Valerie's fund raiser to benefit abused children.

"Just give a holler if you need any help at all, Missy. I'll be right over there," Valerie acknowledged with a nod of her head toward the room's other desk.

Before she completed her steps to the room's other furnishing, she glanced back and noted Missy still appeared curious about something, so she turned and asked, "Is there anything else I can help you with?"

Missy shrugged.   "Well, there is, but I guess it's nothing important. I'm probably just being nosy." She wound a lock of her straight blond shoulder length hair around one of her fingers.

Valerie smiled, and conveyed with a nod she wanted to hear more. Missy continued quietly at Valerie's implied encouragement, "Um, well, it looked like you kinda got lost there for a minute, ya know?"

She hesitated for an instant and continued, "Your face got a spacey look on it. It was like you weren't here at all. Where were you?" Missy's words slipped from where she sat in front of the computer she used.

Valerie's entire essence warmed with the thoughts her imagination so recently indulged in. She hoped her bodily reaction to the man she saw didn't show any worse than it already had. "It was nothing; I just got distracted."

Missy tilted her head toward her and tightened one side of her mouth up, as if in question.

"Um." *She wants to know more. What can I say now?* Valerie diverted her attention to the window. *Honesty's always the best policy.* "Somebody just walked into the auditorium. I didn't expect to see him, I mean, anyone here today. I'm sure Sandy will take care of it." *If she ever gets here.*

Anxiety rampaged Valerie's insides. *I'm sure that door was locked. How'd he get in there?* The awareness she knew the answer intensified her disquiet. She pulled her office chair out and sat in it, lost in her thoughts.

Valerie glanced back out the office's lone window into the auditorium and held her breath. Tightness tickled her. *Why*

do I sense this intimate knowledge with
that stranger?

Chapter Twelve

Although she desired he be the man from her dreams, but discounted it; Valerie wondered at the odds of her running into the same man twice in a day. *I did hire the magician sight unseen. Is it him? Why've I happened upon him twice today?*

Valerie didn't place much substance in coincidence. She rummaged through her recollection to the time of her first contact with his office. It returned to her she didn't even speak with the magician himself at that time.

A female voice, whom she assumed belonged to his secretary, answered her call. She assured Valerie the magician had the dates she inquired about available, and would be happy to work with her. He'd contact her about specifics, later.

Her attention through the window grew more focused. His trademark, the unusual cane in his hands, ascertained his identity as the magician Valerie employed.

The prop he carried appeared with him in all his ads. *It fits his persona.*

She hoped he wouldn't look up and catch her scrutiny of him as her attraction to and admiration of the mystery man grew. His tall body exuded confidence as he breezed across the auditorium's floor.

The suspected magician perused the seating area and scanned the ceiling. He walked down the aisle and up onto the stage. Once there, he knelt and ran his hand over the floor's polished surface.

Valerie's insides entertained hesitation. She didn't know if she felt ready to meet with him again so soon after this morning's chance encounter. *Especially in another such unexpected way.*

She slanted her attention toward the room's door, her eyes fixed in expectation. Valerie hoped her advisor, Sandy, would show up soon. She rubbed her sweaty palms together in her moment of indecision over what she should do while she waited.

Everything inside her, especially something deep down at the very core of her being, wouldn't leave her to sit in silence. She found each breath harder to take than the last. His presence held her spellbound.

He winced and brought his hand back up in front of him with a sharp movement. Valerie likewise experienced discomfort at his sudden action, like a jagged wooden stake pierced through her.

She surged in her seat with the urge to jump up and run to save him. The acute sensation of an ancient memory told her she caused his pain. She released breath she didn't know she held when he put his hand back down and continued his observations.

Valerie knit her eyebrows at her reaction and justified its impulsiveness. *Liability. SCSO, through the church, could be held responsible for his injury. Of course. That's the reason for my quick inclination to be concerned about him.*

She glanced over at the cluttered bulletin board beside her desk in an effort to ground herself and calm her nerves. With the same intention, she also ran her vision around the little room where she sat with Missy.

The work-study student's back faced the volunteer social worker. It gratified Valerie to see Missy busily typed, and paid more attention to the windows on her computer's monitor, than to her.

Valerie smiled appreciatively at the girl. The young high-school student appeared to have no problem with either the office hardware in front of her, or her new data-entry assignment.

Sight of her familiar surroundings relaxed the tension in her chest and reminded Valerie of an important forgotten fact. The manager's booth existed behind a wide mirrored window. She couldn't possibly be seen by the visitor in the auditorium.

The glass barrier between the two of them stretched across the upper back of the church's 5,000 seat auditorium. The marvelous window afforded her the privacy to wipe her brow in relief.

Knowledge she no longer need be

concerned about the magician's awareness as she watched him - and the vantage point of where she sat - endowed Valerie with a powerful sensation of superiority.

She straightened her back and perched forward on her chair. The new position afforded her a keen overview of all the downstairs. She clasped her hands under her chin, supported herself with her elbows, and relaxed in observation.

She couldn't see the bitter distrust she sensed he displayed this morning. A belated afterthought she could've possibly caused that reaction in him, a total stranger, still gave her a sudden jolt of annoyance.

How could he feel that way toward me? He couldn't possibly know me. Even if he did, there'd be no reason for him not to trust me, of all people. She cleared her throat and dropped her hands onto the desk in resignation over her next action.

It seemed their bus station acquaintance would be renewed. At least it lightened her load to know even though she'd hired this year's entertainment; the show's supervision would be someone else's job. *So where is that woman?*

After those few brief moments of deliberation, Valerie leaned into her hands and pushed herself up and away from the desk. The time had come she must abandon her clandestine post of observation.

In an aside as she went to leave the room, she tossed to Missy, "He must be the magician I called about our fundraiser. I'd better go see if I can help him."

Chapter Thirteen

Valerie stopped with her hand on the office's door. For encouragement, she assured herself she wouldn't need to stick around any longer than necessary after her tardy supervisor arrived. She took a deep breath and pulled the door open.

Her nerves inspired slow quiet steps down the stairs. She didn't want to warn him of her approach. The necessity she should be the one to meet with him, at all, clogged her throat at Sandy's absence.

"Where could she be?" she uttered about her supervisor. "This is really odd of that woman. Sandy should be here. I wonder where she could be." With each step she took, Valerie looked less forward to renewed conversation with her visitor.

Her breath came in erratic bursts. She stiffened her back in an effort to gather all the confidence she could muster. It'd be up to her to entertain the man for the moment, and introduce him to Sandy whenever she showed up.

It eased Valerie's mind when she noted the man in the auditorium appeared not to

have noticed her exit from the loft door.
Instead, he remained on his knees and
seemed quite interested in the woodwork of
the stage floor.

Valerie froze in mid-step when the
aisle floor she descended on creaked under
her footstep. Her supposed new hire
glanced up at her from under his brows.
His hand never ceased its sensual caress
across the stage's hardwood floor.

The moment their eyes caught, the
muscles in her most intimate place tensed.
The current between them pulled her toward
him. Vague perceptions of unrecognizable
times passed flashed through her mind.

Valerie's world unfocused. Her
heart fluttered. Her step faltered. She
stood helpless in the charisma of his
magnetic authority. As the seconds ticked
by, she remained entrapped in the
familiarity of her eye-to-eye contact with
him.

The same power, which glued her eyes
to him, kept Valerie on her feet as they
moved her toward where he knelt. An
instance of déjà vu-like nausea engulfed
her at the same time as an inexplicable
wave of guilt billowed through her.

The fault she sensed weighed heavy on
her soul and strengthened with each step
her legs took toward the stage. Just as
quickly as she became trapped in his gaze;
it released her from its grip.

Her power became her own again. She
bathed in the instant of reprieve from the
power he emanated, and regained her
bearings. But the inexplicable guilt
still weakened her spirit.

Valerie didn't want to do this, just

as she sensed she hadn't wanted to do something in a previous time, but she knew she must. An uncertain smile graced her lips as she continued onward.

She still hadn't escaped his rapt attention. It seemed his eyes devoured her. At the same time as she sought to flee his presence, her body once more warmed in the most intimate way it'd taken to betray her with recently.

Valerie's body quivered with vague memory of how his hands once roamed over her body in the same sort of freedom as his eyes now did. She caught herself at that point and reined her imagination in. *I must close my lustful mind's eye. This is business, nothing more.*

Her heart palpitated, but she regained cautious control over herself just before she reached the stage. *You must keep the show in mind, Valerie. That is all you're here for.*

On her arrival at the base of the performance area's imagined front wall, he stood and walked across the shined wood to greet her. He lowered to one knee when they met and gazed down to her.

With one of his arms rested on his bent knee, he waited for her to speak to him. His eyes sparkled down on her as she spoke, "Hello. Are you Mr. Stone?"

"I am. And you are?"

She swallowed and donned her professional appearance. "Valerie Baldwin. I hired you. But I wasn't expecting to see you this morning."

"At the terminal," he inferred. Then, with an I caught you grin, he nodded up toward the window Valerie thought she hid behind, "or from behind that two-way mirrored window?"

Valerie lowered her face. The realization he "caught" her increased the discomfort she experienced. Her face flamed with the heat of her awareness. "You're right on both counts." She willed the floor to open up and swallow her.

The burn on Valerie's face continued its growth. Her moist brow ached to be wiped. She couldn't comprehend how he knew the two-way capability of the window, or that she watched him from behind it when he entered the auditorium.

I'd better not say any more about that before I talk myself into a corner. But she went on anyway. "I guess, what I really meant was, *here.* Now," she added with a sharp poke of a finger to the floor at her feet."

Her face glowed crimson by this time, she knew it. In an attempt to regain her say over this situation, she took his large confident hand in her smaller pampered one and gave it a firm shake.

His hand intimately enfolded hers.

She shivered as she lost control of the circumstances under the dominion his grip implied.

Her insides desired more. She pulled her hand from his in retaliation of her body's betrayal.

Valerie glanced around her shoulder at the large empty room they occupied. She trembled in her situation and locked her arms about themselves. "It's chilly in here, don't you think?" she commented in effort to explain her body's reaction.

He shrugged in what appeared as

indifference, and hopped from his perch on the stage to stand beside her. She experienced every moment of his action, from the push-off of his strong arms to the coordinated balance his long legs offered.

"No, not too," he disagreed. "I'm glad we meet again, Ms. Baldwin." His smooth, low and husky tone revved her hormones.

Valerie froze her expression. She imagined the still shot of her face while her mind raced about in wonder of what she should say next. Truth be told, she wanted him to touch more than her hand.

In the next moment her stomach quivered when the distrustful expression from earlier hastened across his face. Valerie wished she hadn't come out of hiding and told him who she was. She stared at the door to speed Sandy along.

Chapter Fourteen

Valerie's heart shivered with the mysterious knowledge she glimpsed in him. She knew those emotions of his from sometime before. But as he gazed into her eyes, with eyes she assumed saw more than most, she couldn't discern from when or where.

Her head hurt with all the facts she imagined knowledge of about him. They baffled her. He blinked and appeared confused at the way she looked at him. His expression told her he, too, didn't know all he thought he should.

A moment of intuition about the magician she'd hired refreshed Valerie's memory. It told her he'd been about to come on to her as he'd done with innumerable women. *The general consensuses of his way; take 'em and toss 'em - no obligations.*

"Valerie, you say?" escaped his lips on a breath of air. He stilled his face, and by appearances searched hers, with a recognition she couldn't comprehend. "Of course. I should've known. You look like

Valerie."

"Y-e-s." She didn't recognize the voice he employed. It didn't match the one he used when he first acknowledged her presence. It sent shivers through her.

Valerie wondered why he again didn't look like he liked her, or her name. As always before, she could almost see it, but couldn't. Her conception of a certain knowledge, which she couldn't take firm hold of, scared her more than anything else.

He looked upon her with the same perceived hatred and distrust of this morning's chance meeting - if she'd perceived it correctly. His quiet voice also sounded as if he thought her an abomination.

Did she really want to know why he changed so, in the space of an instant, by the sound of her mere name? In spite of herself, she cocked her head and asked, "Is there something wrong with my name?"

He gave his head a quick shake and smiled. His whole persona of the horrible moment before vanished with his earlier expression's return. He took her hand again and gripped it with warmth between both of his. His action tormented her femininity.

His shoulders trembled for an instant before he answered, "No. There's not a thing wrong with your name. Please excuse me. What I meant was that you look like *A* Valerie."

He paused as if about to say something more, but cleared his throat and finished with, "Some women look like other names, but Valerie," he uttered in the low, sexy, and familiar tone she craved to hear, "fits you perfectly."

His expression softened with his smooth and seductive enunciation of her name. The man's warm expression, along with the way her name flowed through his lips, washed a wave of indistinguishable memories through Valerie.

She nimbly slipped her hand from his. Her heart vibrated against her ribs like it beat on a snare drum. Why'd her name on his lips roll off with such a familiar rhythm? With that, she decided the subject couldn't be changed quickly enough, and nodded toward the stage.

"I couldn't help but notice your careful perusal of the auditorium and its stage. Will our arrangements work for your performance?" she asked while she straightened her back and ran her damp palms down her trim thighs.

The magician blinked, and the air of authority he'd arrived with returned. "Yes. This will work. It'll be quite successful for the dynamics of my show."

He sent her a stare she took as over-confidence. "I need to be sure of the proper acoustics and lighting arrangements for my illusions. I'm sure you can understand. What can you tell me about them?"

She imagined he probably didn't think she'd know anything about technical stuff like the theater's audio capabilities. *He probably expects me send him to a man for answers.*

In all actuality, he had her pegged right. Valerie quickly glanced away before she blushed and wished she did know more about what he asked.

Chapter Fifteen

Valerie needed to extricate herself from the situation with as much grace as possible. It placated her to know the person he would talk to about the building was indeed a woman, anyway. *That should show him.*

She gestured to the magician and then around at the lifeless auditorium space around them. "No, Mr. Stone, I can't tell you about the acoustics and lighting arrangements here." She cleared her throat and continued, "That isn't my area.

"Nor is it in my job description." She added in a precise statement. "I'm in charge of this year's entertainment, which apparently is you." She hoped her words portrayed a definite illustration of her importance with his employment at SCSO.

A burst of warm air billowed in and through the atmosphere around them when the door at the room's side opened. "Is this our magician for the show?" Sandy called out to them as she zipped in from outside.

She scurried to the front of the stage

and scooted into place beside Valerie. "I'm so sorry I'm late. Traffic is clogged for miles for what reason I have no idea." She placed a hand to her chest. "It's *never* been this busy!"

Valerie heaved a relieved exhalation. *It's about time, which is not quite perfect.*
She issued her supervisor a grateful smile of relief at her not to timely appearance, and circled one of her hands in Alecksander's direction.

"Yes it is our magician, Sandy. This is Mr. Alecksander Stone." She paused in search of more to say, then smiled and repeated the words in his advertisement. Her finish came out with an exaggerated air of grandeur. "'the Master Magician'."

Valerie turned to her side toward Alecksander and designated Sandy as she spoke, "Mr. Stone, this is Sandy McCoullough. She's the show's supervisor and is the one to whom you should address all your technical questions."

Alecksander and Sandy extended their hands toward each other and exchanged a firm, business-like handshake.

"I was just inquiring of Valerie, um Ms. Baldwin, about the auditorium's lighting," Alecksander began. He Looked to her and asked, "Would it be okay if I used your first name?"

Valerie considered his question and any possible reason for his asking it. "Of course you may. That's why I introduced myself that way." The magician then turned his back on Valerie and began to speak of his business needs with Sandy.

Left out of the conversation like an

unwanted stray, Valerie issued her goodbyes, "I guess I'll be seeing you two sometime later then." Without a moment waited for a response from them, she hustled back to the observation room.

Her back, and everything erogenous in her, warmed as she left. The tension his mention of her name sent through her replayed on her senses. In her mind's eye she envisioned he watched her until she closed the loft door between them.

The conception made her very self-conscious of her movements and she couldn't help but imagine how her departure looked to him. *Did he like what he saw? Did it even matter to him? Should it matter to me?*

As she re-entered the room where the patient Missy waited, Valerie chided her overactive imagination over its "vision" of his lustful look after her, and the effect it exercised on her. *That's just silly.*

"Is he your magician?" Missy drooled to Valerie in an excited breath before her supervisor made it completely into the room.

Valerie latched the door behind her back. "Apparently so," she replied with as much nonchalance as she could muster. "And he's not *my* magician," she added in case Missy guessed her thoughts.

"He's pretty hunky and mysterious, don'cha think?"

Valerie released an inflated sigh of boredom. "As men go."

"What are they talking about?" Missy wondered to Valerie.

"Technical stuff," Valerie answered.

"Lights, sound, stuff like that."

Missy went back to work and tapped a few keys on her keyboard.

"There. I'm all done with my last assignment. What would you like me to do now?" she chirped.

Valerie arched an eyebrow at Missy's brief attention span. "Nothing until we speak further with Sandy."

They both watched the two in the auditorium until he left and Sandy returned to where Valerie and Missy sat in captive audience.

"He watched you leave, Valerie," Sandy suggestively stated when she entered the room. "Did you see?" she inserted with a nod to Missy in reference to the watch she seemed to know they both kept.

"No, I didn't! I missed it!" Missy lamented. "Darn!"

"Are you sure that's what he did?" Valerie wondered.

"Very," Sandy assured her.

Missy heaved a dejected sigh, as if at her missed opportunity. "Well, I guess I'll go out and get my homework now. I'll be right back."

"It seemed he couldn't take his eyes off you," the SCSO supervisor continued. She gave a suggestive raise of her eyebrows to an embarrassed Valerie. "He's a real catch. I'm sure he's interested in you. If you know what I mean."

Sandy elbowed Valerie and ended her move with a suggestive wink. She grinned at the disdainful expression Valerie hurled her way.

Valerie furrowed her brows in mock annoyance at her friend's insinuation.

She remembered the hot picture she'd envisioned of the magician's eyes on her back. It appeared the sensation had obviously been the "third eye" of her intuition.

"Oh?" she asked with effort not to show emotion, and looked down to the pile of fund raiser paperwork on her desk. "Don't be silly. He's interested in all the women." It made Valerie glad Missy missed the latest news Sandy brought in.

The girl struggled in under an armload of high school textbooks and over to an empty desk. She plopped the stack onto her temporary desk. Without a pause for a moment's breath, she asked Sandy, "Wasn't that a yummy looking man?"

Chapter Sixteen

Sandy nodded, tilted her head in Valerie's direction, and asked, "What do *you* think about your magician, Valerie?"

"He's not *my* magician," Valerie corrected. "Why do you all insist on thinking that?" she queried without an immediate lapse in attention to her work. When she did raise her head, two noncommittal faces stared back at her in mock innocence.

Missy broke the charade first. "You have all the luck, Valerie! Where did you find him? Does he have any brothers?" She blurted everything she said in one breath as if she couldn't hold it in one moment longer.

Valerie encountered Missy's questions head-on. "What do you mean, I 'have all the 'luck'?" *It's not like I've had any dates, lately.* "He just happens to be the magician I hired who chose this afternoon to appear here. No pun intended.

"And furthermore, I don't have any idea if he has any brothers. You can have *him*, if you want. I'm not interested." She waved the back of her hand toward Missy in illustration and returned her attention to the documentation on her desk.

But even for all the effort she gave, Valerie's mind wouldn't return to its focus on her paperwork. Instead, her thoughts returned to the distrust she'd witnessed in the magician's eyes. It plagued her sanity.

Valerie tingled with the unrequited sexual excitement his familiar eyes inspired in her. She peered at Missy from under her brow. "I don't think he liked me, anyway."

A brief expression of hot opportunity flashed across Missy's wide-eyed face before she sobered and examined her fingernails. With what appeared as disinterest, she asked, "Um, why not?"

Valerie arched an eyebrow at the expression of fair game that passed - like a hunter after prey - across Missy's face. "I'm sure I have no idea why not," she responded. "Doesn't matter anyway. He's not my type."

She imagined Missy a little too young for the magician, whom she assumed had at least a good ten years on her. But she couldn't help the thought her mind entertained. *Go for it, Missy.*

Valerie shook with her perception of the magician's mistrust of her. It irritated her the distinct impression wouldn't leave her be. *There's no reason for him not to like or trust me. We don't even know each other, for Heaven's Sake.*

It has to be something in our chemistry somewhere that gives him his cause. That, she reasoned, would be the only rational reason for his sometimes cold attitude toward her. *He's shallow, like most "to die for" men tend to be.*

Valerie switched her frown at her judgment of him to a poker-face and hoped her feelings hadn't betrayed themselves to her co-workers. She rifled through some desk-top documents and continued with her best efforts to concentrate on the text.

"Talk to Sandy if you want to know more about the magician."

Sandy piped up at Valerie's instruction with a lilt that teased. She directed it to their young work study student, "He should be here in a few minutes, Missy."

Valerie's stomach flip-flopped in anticipation. She thought of how she'd love to be on friendlier terms with Alecksander. *But why, when I know we've never met, do I feel like I've known and hurt him in the past?*

****

Alecksander stepped from his luxurious car in front of the church offices. He paused before he entered and put a hand on his chin. *Where do I know that Valerie woman from?*

Memory of their brief acquaintance at the bus terminal subliminally passed through his consciousness. A note in the back of his mind prodded him. Alecksander understood he knew her from much longer ago than he'd imagined, but not from where.

A hint flashed through his mind. It appeared as if a forgotten memory, which sped through in an instant of agonized clarity. He choked and his body stiffened, as if impaled on a stake.

Alecksander stretched and flexed to

rid himself of the imagined moment of
pain. He conceived his body's reaction to
his desire of her forewarned him, of what he
didn't know. It verified his earlier
decision. *I shouldn't trust her.* But he
wanted to.

From that moment; he couldn't be at
rest.
His head ached as his reliable pit of the
gut feeling - which he always listened to
- set in. He argued with it. *Maybe it
wouldn't be so bad if I ignored my
intuition for this one time only.*

Alecksander put his palms on his back
and massaged. His discomfort made its
point about whatever it warned him about.
But Valerie affected him in a different
way than the other women in his past. She
just felt so meant to be for him.

He wanted her much more and for
longer than any other of his conquests.
Maybe he *could* trust her, if he gave her
the chance. Still, the sensation in the
pit of his gut remained. It niggled
against his stubbornness and warned she'd
hurt him.

Just as she already has? The
workings of his inner-mind endeavored to
convince him she varied little from the
rest.   In the end he compromised and
assured himself he wouldn't let his guard
down around her.

He leaned back against his shiny black
late-model Mercedes Benz and rubbed his
palms down the sides of his face. Nothing
he did helped his condition. His headache
worsened with the haze of scattered
memories the woman stirred in him.

Alecksander ached to pound his fists

into his brain. Why couldn't he clearly
recall its vague visions?

Chapter Seventeen

Alecksander wondered what Valerie did when not at work. He wondered if a man of interest existed in her life. The imagined possibility of someone else with her stirred passionate jealousy in him.

Alecksander focused, straightened in renewed self-discipline, and strode with rekindled vigor to the institution in front of him. A spidery sensation crawled through his chest as he stood outside the office he knew Valerie worked in.

He opened the building's door and slipped inside with a failed stealth tactic. Ms. McCoullough immediately approached him and issued greetings. Her smile and friendly voice welcomed him.

"There you are. Welcome to our office. I have the paperwork you need to complete for us over here, Mr. Stone."

He didn't see Valerie in the impromptu gaze he passed over the small lobby they occupied. The supervisor's instructive notification broke his thought about whether he'd see Valerie again, and drew his direct attention.

In passing; he noted a pretty young

woman who flashed him a hesitant yet predatory smile full of semi-straight white teeth. The rapacious beam the girl assaulted him with portrayed itself as above and beyond the call of polite friendliness.

Always on the lookout for a new conquest – like a hunter - Alecksander gave brief consideration to any possibilities with her. It didn't take him long to reach his assumption; the attractive young woman couldn't be more than her late teens.

Too young for me. She seemed more than willing for Alecksander's attentions, as did most of the women he encountered. But he couldn't afford to give them to this one.

The girl quickly returned her attention to her desk and set her pen to a conspicuously rapid pace. It seemed she did so when she realized he gave his attention to her.

Ms. McCoullough appeared to notice their brief exchange and designated the girl to him. "Oh. This is Missy. She's our work-study student from the local high school." Missy smiled through closed lips, nodded to them, and returned to her work.

Alecksander followed another descriptive wave of Ms. McCullough's hand, and stepped into her office. She spoke as they entered the room. "I'm glad you're willing to work with us on an agreeable fee for your services, Mr. Stone.

"Since we're going to be spending a lot of time together in this show's production; from now on let's operate strictly on a first name basis. Please, call me Sandy."

"You can call me, Alecksander." He pulled out his chair from in front of her desk and sat after Sandy eased down into hers behind the desk. He then took up the pen she offered him and waited for her to give him something to sign.

As Alecksander gazed mindlessly at the forms she placed in front of him, his mind rambled in a way he couldn't control. He wondered where Valerie could be. *I wish she were the one I could do all this with.*

His gut twisted on him. He both needed to know more about her, and didn't want to. He glanced up to Sandy while couched in his dilemma. She appeared as if she speculated at his expression. The look on her face snapped him to out of his reverie.

He held no desire to give this supervisor the wrong impression about his personal intentions. He signed and proceeded to fill out the proffered forms as quickly as possible.

The unusual situation Alecksander found himself in with Valerie, stumped him. Her image prioritized itself over all else in his mind. *Women don't affect me this way.* He saw the paperwork before him, but couldn't take his mind off Valerie.

Where do I know her from? Why do I feel so familiar with her? Why does she both frighten and excite me?

He couldn't help but wish Valerie would put down her guard and call him Alecksander, in the soft seductive way he somehow knew only she could. Lustful adrenalin coursed through him at his uncanny knowledge of the gentleness her voice could possess.

He forced his focus. While a part of his mind buzzed through the legalities the paperwork needed, his rebellious memory refused to forget his acquaintance with Valerie, no matter what.

Chapter Eighteen

Why don't I feel I can trust her, or any woman, for that matter?
Alecksander dropped his pen. Shocked, he glanced up and saw no awareness of it from Sandy. A like sound from the other room caught his ear, and for a moment renewed his thought to the girl, but again he dismissed her.

Even though Sandy's and Missy's attractiveness caught his eye, Valerie alone ensnared his desires. *I don't even know her well enough for that.* But his subconscious continued at him with gave him cause for reconsideration. *Or do I?*

He noted Valerie's chair sat empty when they left the office space. *Where is she?* He paused for a moment of speculation in a warm spot of sunlight at the front window. The cheerfulness it offered calmed his inner turmoil.

Alecksander turned to face the two women when he heard the mention of Valerie's name. It appeared they were about to inadvertently answer his questions about her.

"Where's Valerie gone to?" Sandy asked Missy.

"Ya got me," Missy responded. The girl flicked one of her hands back and forth in illustration. "She's been in and out. Actually, you just missed her. She did some stuff while you visited with the magician, then left."

"Where'd she go?" Sandy asked.

Missy shrugged. "I don't know. She murmured something about how she needed to get out of here, had to be somewhere for something very important, or something like that. And she said she'd be gone for the rest of the day."

The girl's eyes darted over to Alecksander several times while she spoke. At the end of her hurried answer, she sent a sweet smile over to him where he stood at the window by the doorway.

Alecksander immediately cast his gaze outward.

****

The lock indicator on the driver's side door of Valerie's car clicked up as she approached it in the church parking lot. Her heart skipped a beat and she froze. Breath escaped her. Jagged spears of adrenaline spiked through her ears.

She stared at the unused car keys in her hand. Her recent actions replayed themselves in her mind. *I didn't press the remote control button by accident, did I?*

No one else would have a remote to my car, could they? Valerie craned her head around *in* search of a likely culprit. She never considered someone else might have one, but with all the computer hackers around, it could happen.

Valerie didn't see anyone nearby she would suspect in her investigation, so she assumed the responsibility for her surprise as her own. Even so, anxious nerves tingled on the top of her head with her next consideration.

There could still be someone, whom she couldn't see, inside the car. Her heart fluttered. Valerie stood on her tiptoes and arched her neck toward the vehicle, as if she peered over into the depths of a canyon.

The action of closer inspection did her no good. She still couldn't see the car's floorboard across the vacant car space between herself, and her little Honda Accord.

It frustrated her she couldn't see below where the window met the car's shiny silver painted door. She frowned and wished she had x-ray vision to see through the metal frame. *Could someone possibly be hiding inside my car?*

Valerie's eyes locked and she stared into space. Should she turn back and enlist the assistance of the ground's guard? She decided to continue on with no intentions to play the part of the hapless heroine today.

In the day's brightness, Valerie figured it'd be okay. Any call for help she made would alert her co-workers. *Who in his right mind would try to accost me at this place and time of day? That sort of person* wouldn't *be in his right mind.*

Her final thought upset her nerves even more, yet she continued her pace. Her heart skipped a few beats and she gasped when the car's door opened before her hand reached its handle.

The car's floorboard now lay clearly visible to her. She saw no one on it. If someone in there opened the door for her, that "someone" would have to be on the floor in the front of the car; wouldn't they? *Where are they?*

She inched closer to her car, certain of someone's presence in it and careful to make no more noise than absolutely necessary. In this fashion, she fully expected to be able to catch the guilty party unaware of her cognizance.

At her Honda's side, Valerie peered over into it, but still didn't see anyone. At that point she relaxed as best as she could, despite the way her heart pounded, until tiny pinpricks gathered on her shoulders.

They prickled up her neck to her ears. *Uncanny wouldn't be the word used to describe my situation. Something supernatural would be a better term.* She spun on her heels. The time arrived she should turn and get that guard.

The back of Alecksander's gold emblazoned on black suit presented itself to her through the window when she turned. Attraction sparked through her at its beckon.

Chapter Nineteen

Alecksander turned his attention out the window. It seemed he fully expected her gaze. He smiled, gave her a polite nod and another brief raise of his eyebrow, and faced back inside.

Did he open my door? Her eyes widened when the remembrance of the way he'd appeared - and disappeared - at the bus terminal beset her. She placed a hand over her opened mouth.

"Oh. My. Goodness. He did. He opened my door," she exclaimed under her breath.

The man is truly an anomaly. She gripped her car keys firmly and turned to go back to her car.

It took her a moment to slip the car's shiny silver key into the ignition. Under her shaky grip; the small tool scraped back and forth around the keyhole until at length it slipped in.

At her first turn of the key, the engine began its soothing mechanical hum. The sound gave Valerie the peace of escape she needed and she sank down into the soft fabric upholstery of its bucket seat with relief.

Then she glanced back to the office window and saw the man stood there no more. *His interest in me has once more obviously waned.* She wished she'd see more sustained personal interest in those irresistible liquid brown eyes of his.

A week later, Valerie woke from a fitful night's sleep with tears in her eyes. She rubbed them and frowned at herself. *Why am I crying over a dream?* She caught her breath as she realized she'd dreamt of life with the magician in the old west.

Did it really happen? I've heard of other people discussing past lifetimes. Could I have lived before, too? With him? She shook her head. Valerie's strict sense of reality couldn't believe that.

She'd thought to have her alarmingly accurate sense of empathic perception under control. Her gift remained kept in check as she only consciously used it with the children she helped, until the magician appeared in her life.

Since that time she'd begun to dream of people other than the little ones who needed her help. She now also dreamed of other lifetimes. Valerie attempted to shake the new reality of her dreams off as she climbed from her bed.

Valerie wrapped in her bathrobe and padded into the room's adjacent bathroom. The shower's water warmed quickly onto her hand, and she shook her robe off her shoulders.

She reached behind herself to hang her housecoat, and entered past the curtain with little thought of her effort. A soft frump on the floor told her she'd missed the hook.

With no further thought to the matter, Valerie stood directly under the water's spray. It massaged her to further wakefulness and pounded the uneasiness of her dreams away.

* * * *

"Hey! I know you've had your fill of women who were only after the title of being seen on your arm. But maybe this," Clarke emphasized the word with his hands firmly placed on the table between him and Alecksander.

"Is the woman you've waited for. Let down your guard and ask her out." Alecksander's friend, a former Army drill sergeant, issued his final sentence in a way that sounded more like an order than a friendly suggestion.

Alecksander gave his head a slow nod as he evaluated his friend's advice. He also noted the attention his friend's strong voice drew from the coffee shop's other patrons, which he ignored.

He patted his palms face down on the air in front of him in effort to calm Clarke's enthusiasm. "Relax. I've been thinking I might just do that. When I first got to this town, something told me when I finally met someone, she'd be from here.

"I don't know why that thought flashed through my head. I still don't know if I'm ready for a real relationship, or if it should be with her. What I do know is I don't want to jump into anything just because of my crazy imagination."

The magician paused and shot a guarded look at Clarke, who appeared ready to pounce. "Okay, I'll admit there is something about the aura that developed between me and that woman when we first met.

"It both warned me away from her and presented me with an irresistible attraction to her the same time." He rubbed his chin between his fingers. "I don't understand my reaction to it."

"She scared ya, huh?" Clarke teased with a suggestive wink.

Alecksander gazed off into space and softly uttered, "Yes, I confess. She scared me. It frightened me when I envisioned what she held for me."

Clarke's eyebrows raised in a sarcastic expression.

"Control yourself, Clarke. The vision I received portrayed itself as sheer agony." A quick shiver racked the self-composed magician's body. He shook it off and regained his strength without any conscious betrayal of it to his friend.

"Listen to me. Look at *me*. My unintended meeting with that woman has got me acting like a moron!" When he saw Clarke's mouth begin to form another sarcastic reply, he quickly held his fisted hand up for silence.

"Don't start. Do Not Start," Alecksander reiterated. You don't want to mess with me at this moment," he growled through a grin.

Clarke closed his mouth and pulled his chin in. He straightened in self-defense

and held his hands up in a mock
illustration of surrender. Then he
returned Alecksander's grin and defended in
denial, "I didn't say a thing."

"No, you didn't. But I heard those
loose cogs in your brain turning. You
thought about it."

Chapter Twenty

Her concentration left her; life-like dreams consumed her. Valerie bumped into the frame of SCSO's office door when she arrived for her day's work. Threads of the magician tightly bound her thoughts to him alone.

She peered around to see if anyone witnessed her moment of clumsiness. All morning she'd relived the magic he already brought into her life, and wondered what other types of trickery he kept under his sleeves. *Does he know my thoughts?*

She placed one of her hands to her forehead and closed her eyes. *Oh no. There I go again. Why can't I trust him?* Her inability to form a trusting, loving bond with another had left her lonely for what seemed like forever.

After Valerie reached her small office space without any further mishap, she relaxed back into her chair. Her eyes caught on the oil on canvas painting of a beautiful pond on the wall across from her desk. The picture's ambience soothed her.

She relaxed into her comfortable

chair. It gratified her SCSO allowed her choice of office furniture and decorations when the organization remodeled. She noticed no calls on her agenda, which meant she could react to events as they came.

Valerie tilted her head back and closed her eyes for a brief moment of relaxation. *BRING!* She jolted upright and almost out of her chair when the phone rang. Her mind alerted from its moment of rest and returned to its professional status.

"Sunview Children's Services organization. This is Valerie Baldwin speaking. How may I help you this morning?" An anonymous caller alerted her to a child's suspected abuse, and she knew her day's first assignment would be field work.

Valerie ended the call with a click of a button and glanced at the time on her phone. She hoped she'd be able to later make a prompt arrival for the first performance of their current fundraiser.

Her obligation didn't work out to be a case of genuine child abuse. Its false alarm eased her soul. Valerie's heart broke on each occasion field work called her out, yet her psyche summoned her to where children needed her presence.

She returned to her office where she completed the required data entry on her morning mission. After she finished, Valerie saw she still had time to make the performance. She grabbed her purse, locked the door and headed down to the auditorium.

"The feat The Master Magician will attempt tonight has never been accomplished - successfully - before." The loudspeaker's voice paused; the air in the room chilled.

The crowd hushed and the diabolical disembodied voice continued with a whispered tone into the audience's silence, "The torture box on the stage, which The Master Magician will enter in a few moments, is laced with steel spikes."

The unseen speaker spoke with drawn out essss sounds. Panic-stricken alarm curled through Valerie, and she assumed the others who listened to him, as well. Silence ensued.

Two well-poised young women dressed in golden gowns, which flowed in layered waves to the floor, entered onto the stage. Each evening dress glittered out to the spectators in a precious golden array.

The ladies gracefully opened the up-ended coffin-shaped box. They pointed to the silver spikes of deadly pins as the announcer spoke. The ominous spears appeared as numerous needles, which hungrily awaited a pin cushion.

The seemingly braver of the two ladies onstage placed a ginger tap of an index finger to one of the pins. She jerked her fingertip back and tenderly placed it between her pouty red lip-sticked lips.

Her partner in the show hopped a step back toward the rear of the stage with one of her hands over her mouth. She gasped and stared at the other as if in shock her partner would even imagine to do such a dangerous thing.

"Ahh!" Valerie and the others with her sucked in their breath in unison. Everyone cringed and pressed back into their seats. Defensive hands covered faces as if in dread of what danger the Master Magician would place himself in.

The speaker system's eerie voice continued, "A contraption such as this would pierce the life out of us. Let's watch as The Master Magician enters it and motions for the door to be closed on him by these two lovely ladies."

Alecksander then strode out from the illusive magical colorations of the stage drapes and made his bold entrance onto the stage. He carried his gold tipped black cane and wore his golden laced black suit.

The magician appeared to give no obvious notice to the danger he placed himself in. He stepped inside the box with an air of indifference - and motioned for his beautiful young assistants to close it on him.

"No!" Valerie screamed, to no avail. She couldn't remember this from his practice performances. "This wasn't supposed to be a part of your show!" She held her breath and prayed for his safety.

Chapter Twenty-One

The two young women balked at his suggestion and threw their hands over their faces in signs of horror. It seemed they wished Alecksander hadn't entered the box. Renewed gasps rose from the audience.

Valerie's face chilled as she watched in wide-eyed disbelief. *This can't be real. It has to be an act.*

The Master Magician smiled to everyone. He nodded, as if in assurance he possessed total control. Everything would proceed as he expected.

A breeze whistled across the stage. Those in the front row especially experienced its chill. Everyone in the audience straightened. It seemed as if the air's temperature chilled the spines of all in attendance.

Valerie couldn't move. She could only watch as the stage-girls pushed the heavy doors of the horrible contraption in on her man of magic.

The current of air, which still filtered its way across the stage, lifted the long silky skirts the two attendants

wore. It revealed glimpses of their long
tanned legs, as if in tease.

The box door latched. The air filled
with a muted distorted sound of liquid
release. Reddish liquid seeped from the
body-box.

"Oh, my, God!" Valerie screamed. She
threw herself out of her seat and ran to
the stage. A stage-hand at the bottom of
the stage's stairs grabbed her.

"Sorry, ma'am. I've been instructed
not to allow any interference with the
magician's performance," he informed.

A groan distorted the
auditorium's silence. Spectator
screams echoed through the theatre. The
magician's panicked assistants fumbled with
the box and attempted to free him. The
loudspeaker's voice began again - his tone
changed from its previous nature.

"That agonized sound! Has yet another
magician succumbed to the rigors of this
magical accomplishment? He was supposed
to have vanished before the box closed in
on him! Get that box opened!" it demanded.

"Someone call the Para-Medics!" the
stage-girls screamed over their shoulders
to the hands back stage.

Please, God! Don't let this be so!
Valerie covered her face and hid from the
sight sure to be soon revealed. Her heart
squeezed at the silenced sound in the
auditorium.

She imagined everyone covered their
faces when she did. *No one could possibly
want to see what's happened to
Alecksander.* The box door creaked open.
Valerie's insides froze with the sound.

"He's gone!" the voice from the

theater's sound system declared.

Valerie peeked through her fingers, and then gave her full wide-eyed attention back to the death trap in the center of the stage. The young women onstage peered into the opened cadaver-sized box. Their expressions showed wide-mouthed amazement.

A few tentative claps emerged from the silence, a few more followed and soon a roar of applause erupted from the audience. "He's escaped!" they shouted.

Valerie's heart elated. "He's gone!" She shot her vision to all corners of the stage and the auditorium. *But where is he? Where'd he go?*

★★★★

Days later Valerie pushed the door with her foot and left it open behind her when she entered her condo. "A-h-h-h," she moaned as she dropped her brief case with lap-top onto her faux onyx coffee table and collapsed onto her couch.

She still wondered where Alecksander went after he escaped, and why she hadn't heard from him. *His absence must be for publicity, but he hasn't even picked up his check.*

Certain he'd eventually show up, she couldn't be bothered with his elusiveness at the moment. She just needed to get off her feet. "It feels so good to be home." Her spine ached.

She stretched her arms up and out, straightened her back and strained her shoulders back for relief. Her feet throbbed, so she kicked them up onto the small table in front of her.

Valerie glanced back to her door and moaned. *I forgot to close the door.*

She tensed to stand and close the door when a pair of strong hands prevented her from doing so. They kneaded her shoulders between their fingers with magical majesty. She jumped. The physical contact at first startled her. "Ah!" she squealed. But she soon relaxed and enjoyed erotic warmth as it flowed through her.

Valerie knew whose hands delivered such delightful relaxation to her tired and achy body. The enchantment his hands worked on her tired muscles soothed and excited her from head to toe.

She squeezed her shoulders up and back and moaned in ecstasy, "Hi, Alecksander. Where've you been? You scared everyone at your performance."

"You know a magician has his secrets. I didn't mean to startle you when I first came in," he softly intoned. "And I hope you don't mind I entered without invite.

Your door stood open," He offered in explanation, "when I arrived, and there you were. I knew what you wanted as soon as I saw you collapse onto your couch."

"But how did you," she reiterated about his performance.

"A magician has his secrets," he repeated as he cut her sentence off.

Valerie sighed and rolled to her stomach on the cushioned piece of furniture she lay on. She willingly let the magic of his touch take her over.

He continued his charm on her shoulders. Then his touch moved down to her back and across to her sides. His hands traveled perilously close to her breasts, but then changed their direction.

A let down sensation cooled Valerie's

98

warmth when his ministrations stopped at
the sides of her breasts and didn't proceed
any further. They instead returned to the
lower portion of her back and on down to
her legs.

He eased her shoes off and his motions
finished with her foot pads. When he took
the delight of his hands away, her whole
body experienced a magical relief from the
long day spent on her feet.

"You make me feel so special," she
murmured from the half sleep he'd lulled
her to.

"You are."

She kept her eyes closed as she
smiled. "Mmmm. How special am I?" Her
whole body warmed with his ministrations.
She smiled when his lips brushed her neck.
He nibbled on her ear lobes and set her
bodily juices a flow.

Valerie expected more, but nothing
followed. She connected with him in that
moment and saw the reason for the
cessation of his erotic massage. He
feared any further commitment with her.
She searched, but his reason for worry
eluded her.

"Why do you fear," Valerie opened her
eyes and found herself alone in her condo.
She still lay on her couch, and the door
still hung open to the now darkened
outside.

Was I asleep? Valerie ached to think
it'd all been a dream. She wanted
Alecksander. She longed for him night
after night to be at her side. By all his
mannerisms it seemed he wanted her, too.

Her rationalism left her senseless.
She decided she no longer cared about his

haughty mannerisms and surrendered to her
love for him. The possibility of any
future relationship between them would
require counsel.

"Why is he afraid?" she whispered to
herself.

Chapter Twenty-Two

A blurred memory of traumatic circumstances haunted Alecksander. He left Valerie because of it. *I must keep control of our relationship. That's the only way I won't be hurt again.*

****

With each day passed since Alecksander's incredible show; Valeric smiled with gratefulness of how he dazzled with his performance for her and the children's benefit. Her wildest dreams couldn't match the funds raised with the show's success.

Though they'd not sold many advance tickets, non-advance ticket buyers showed up in droves, and paid to enter just before the show began. Those higher priced after-sale entrance fees cost more, from which SCSO derived its profits. *As if by magic.*

After several weeks passed, Valerie knew she needed to do more than think about what a great job the magician did. The obligatory thing for her to do would be to contact and issue personal thanks to him for all he'd done for her organization.

Her stomach jittered with the thought of contacting Alecksander. She'd not heard from him other than in her dream, but she picked up the office phone and dialed his number, anyway. *It is part of my job.*

"Stone here," he answered.

"Alecksander?" she inquired.

"That would be me."

Valerie's fingernails dug into the palms of her hands at his show of arrogance. *He sounds as if he doesn't even know me.* She fought to keep her annoyance with him out of her voice. *I must keep this call impersonal.* "This is Valerie Baldwin.

"I don't know what happened to you, or where you've been. I'm just calling to inform you that our fund-raiser was a success, and to thank you for staging it for us. Why haven't you contacted us for payment since you disappeared?"

"Thank you. It was a pleasure and an honor to work with you. I don't expect payment. Consider it a donation." The flat tone of his voice held no familiarity.

She wondered about his denial of payment for his services, but of more importance, Valerie's inner-ear heard the trauma he endured.

His tone beseeched her for help. *But how can I help him? He's a grown man. He might not appreciate my dragging up his past history.*

"Um, I was hoping we here at Children's Services might be able to work together with you on future show arrangements."

"That is entirely possible."

"Of course, we *would* need to reimburse you for your services at those times."

"Perhaps."

Valerie tightened her chin and reconsidered her empathy toward him. *His arrogance is unbearable.* She knew she'd probably regret getting involved in his problems, but his past gave her no other choice.

He must come to terms with his bygone days. His wounds need to be healed before he can go forward. She nodded to herself. *That would probably be the best thing for both of us.*

"I'm glad you feel that way," she said into her phone.

"Why don't you come by my office later today, and we'll discuss it," he suggested.

Why don't I go to his office later?

Her nerves did crazy things inside her as she accepted.

★★★★

The interior of "Alecksander Stone's Magical Menagerie," fascinated Valerie. Its variety of diverse and mysterious props, and allusions of the legerdemain its interior held, figuratively leapt out at her.

Charismatic colors on the walls swept excited anticipation through her. She trembled with excitement as her inner child reveled in the fantastic realms promised by everything around her.

The room's contents changed with each minute as it passed. Colors Valerie believed she perceived on the walls blended like a kaleidoscope into other

shades. It especially intrigued her when
those shades matched and coordinated with
separate articles of her clothing.

Props and displays continually
morphed into various but distinct forms of
other like items. She felt like one
with the room, but shivered in the
supernatural atmosphere of all she found
herself surrounded by.

"How do you like it?" a voice echoed.

Valerie's skeletal system jumped as
if in escape mode from her skin. Her
heart pounded. The voice she heard
sounded like it came from nowhere - and
everywhere. She wondered at the question
she heard in the room where she thought
herself alone.

The pound of her heart skipped and she
lost her breath when she turned and found
herself face-to-face with Alecksander.
He'd positioned himself across the narrow
aisle from where she stood.

Valerie gasped and threw one of her
hands to her chest. "Goodness Sakes!
Where'd you come from?" she asked him.

He rubbed his chin. "Here. I've
watched you this entire time. I enjoy
observing people and their reactions when
they enter my shop for the first time."

She swept her gaze wandered around
her. "This is all so magical and
misleading, and exciting!" she chattered,
but quickly closed the door on her inner
child-like animation and regained her
professional demeanor as quickly as
possible.

She cleared her throat, "Ahem. I
mean, it's very curious. Your shop
brings many wonders to my mind, but," she

said as she pushed all her awe aside with a hand, "you can tell all you have to say about it, later. We have business to discuss right now."

An impish grin covered Alecksander's face. "I never divulge my secrets," he reminded her.

She nodded in remembrance. "Of course. Is there someplace here where we can sit and talk about future engagements?" Her face warmed and she quickly added, "Um, I mean, for my organization's shows?"

The magician gave his right eyebrow a quick raise and turned. "Come with me into my office."

Said the spider to the fly.

He waited at the inconspicuous door - amidst all the shop's illusions - to a room for her to enter first. He closed the door behind them and Valerie found them alone together in a much more intimate space.

She battled for self-control in the sensual warmth of the drape covered walls and plush carpets, which surrounded her. She again cleared her throat and began, "SCSO has a Christmas event planned. We'll need entertainment for it.

"The show, of course, won't be for fund-raising. Given the time of year, it will be for donations; toys, clothes, and the like. Would you be interested in again mesmerizing our audience at that time, for us?"

Chapter Twenty-Three

Alecksander moved in silence to his
desk and clicked open his computer
calendar. "What're the dates you're
looking at?"

"The first weekend in December,"
Valerie answered. "That'll give us time
to allocate the gifts out to the needy
before Christmas."

Valerie's cell phone rang and she
turned her attention to it while the
magician checked out his free dates. She
heard his response to her, but ignored him
as she placed her phone to her ear for an
instant and stated, "Yes. I'll be there
quickly."

Her attention returned to Alecksander
as she gathered up her purse and prepared
to leave his office without any further
time spent. "I'm sorry, but I must leave.
It's urgent. You were saying?"

"That date will work fine for me. Is
there anything else I can do for you?" he
asked with a suggestive wink.

Her insides tingled at his
insinuation, but she continued her

preparation for departure, "Not at the moment. I'm sorry, but there's an emergency with one of my children and I really must leave."

"Perhaps we can meet at some other time, then?" His return smile spoke to her of the many sensual things he implied.

Her hormones sustained their relentless race at his query. *This case-call couldn't have come at a better time.* At the last minute she decided on something he *could* do for her, "Well, on second thought, there is something you can do for me."

Her face warmed at the way her thoughts ran. Valerie averted her attention from him and pretended to search through her digital file for something. She closed it without having retrieved a thing, and returned her concentration to her hire.

"We have other dates approaching, during which we do fund-raising activities. I'd like to talk to you about them, but I really do have to run. Maybe we can meet at another time," she stated on a breath of air as she made her way to the door.

"Over coffee, perhaps?"

Valerie's steps stilled. His chosen place sounded innocent enough. It could possibly lead to her knowing more about his past. *He needs to be released from that trauma.* She also sensed she needed to be the one who did it for him.

"I'll call," she said as she darted out, before she again became entrapped in his intrigue. She stopped after she closed his door into a barrier between them.

Her heart beat like she had some silly school-girl crush going on. She tossed her head. *I'm much more grown up than that.* Though it sounded harmless, why he wanted to meet her someplace for coffee instead of in his office puzzled her.

Did he just ask me out for a date? What should she wear? She chuckled, shook her head at the thought. *I've got other business besides you to attend to, Mr. Magician.*

★★★★

Alecksander studied Valerie's departure from his office with untamed interest. His reaction puzzled him. *Why'd I ask her out for coffee? No way do I want to spend any more time with that woman than I have to.* He peered into his misted orb of answers and meditated on it.

★★★★

She didn't call Alecksander for the remainder of that day. At court, too much else occupied her mind on ways she could correct little Katie's situation. Her efforts earned her a successful day in court. It called for a celebration.

"Congratulations, Valerie!" Carol, one of her co-workers exclaimed when a brightened Valerie arrived back at SCSO headquarters after her court date.

"Thanks! Good news travels fast, huh!" she responded while the two hugged.

"Now that she is out of her abusive situation, we need to find Katie a good home where she'll be loved unconditionally," Carol announced.

Valerie remembered Katie's request to go home with her. She would've loved to take the little girl, and all the other

108

children she saved, home with her. As a single woman, though, she knew she'd be the last considered for permanent placement.

She considered the Organization's priority, which was to place unwanted children into two parent homes. The rule for such placement went unsaid. It existed for the implied security such well-rounded homes offered to the children involved.

"Yeah," she replied with less enthusiasm involved in the word, than she'd felt on arrival.

"Oh, she wanted to go home with you, didn't she?" Sandy, who'd just happened into the office, commiserated.

Valerie gave her supervisor a forlorn nod. "Yes. She did."

"What'd you say to her? She's such a loving child. It must've been hard to console her."

"I told her I'd do my best. That was all I could say to her."

Sandy fisted her hand and pounded the air to her side. "And you will do your best. You always do your best." she enthusiastically assured her dispirited worker. "It's not your fault that you're among the last to be considered for placement.

"Your name is on the potential adoptee list for every child we save, and that is the best you can do, just like you told your little charge you'd do.

"Not to change the topic of our conversation, but," she elbowed Valerie before she continued, "have you contacted that new magician boyfriend of yours, yet? This would be cause for a celebration between you two!"

"He's *not* my boyfriend," Valerie flatly reminded her.

"That's what *she* said," Sandy teased. "I've seen the fire between you two when you're in the same room. It leaves me gasping for water."

Valerie relished that 'fire'. It warmed her like she'd never imagined before. "Other than the fact I've hired him to be our next entertainer, and have mentioned future arrangements with him, we're not much more than acquaintances," she lamented.

"Hang in there," Sandy counseled. She gave Valerie another poke in the ribs with her elbow and suggested, "Let's you, me, and Carol go out someplace and celebrate SCSO's successful day in court today."

Chapter Twenty-Four

Valerie considered the fact of Missy's name not on the list Sandy suggested. She glanced to the corner where the student worked. The girl appeared to either be a good actress or hadn't overheard the plans. *I'm sorry you're too young for drinks, Missy.*

She put the day's digital file into her desk drawer. Along with it went her down mood over the court's future placement of Katie, and any concern she had over her questionable relationship with Alecksander.

"How are you doing over there?" Sandy asked Missy.

"Not quite finished, but almost!" the teen-ager sang out. "Well, it's the end of the day. We're all heading out and I believe you should, too. You can put what you're working on aside until you return tomorrow and finish it then."

Missy looked up from her computer and smiled. "Okay. Thanks!" She grabbed her books and headed out the door. "See ya!"

The three women grabbed their purses and followed Missy out. Sandy remained until last, turned off the lights, and left for a Ladies' night with her two friends.

Valerie enjoyed her life immensely when she could be involved in saving a child from a life of misery. A nice dinner and drinks out with her friends, was a perfect way to celebrate her victories.

They could just be themselves on such occasions. No need to worry about impressing or entertaining a man. *Just perfect. Carefree nights like this make my life as a single woman worth it.*

"But what about Alecksander?" Sandy asked, as if she read Valerie's mind. "Aren't you even going to call and tell him about your day?"

"Why tell him? He's just our entertainer. I'll tell him when we meet to talk more about fundraisers."

Their next meeting ~

Valerie purposefully arrived earlier than the magician at Harold's Coffee Shop on the day of their appointed meeting. She meant to discuss her upcoming needs for SCSO with him, and nothing more.

He distracted her to no end. Her early arrival ensured she received focused time to gather her thoughts about the key points she needed to express, while they met.

The mood of the shop changed while Valerie ruminated. She looked up into the room's hush. It appeared the transformation everyone experienced happened when the business' door opened for the magnetic magician's entrance.

Every female eye in the room glued to him when Alecksander arrived on the small social scene in all his magical majesty.

His dress consisted of his trademark cloak and tall black boots. His gold adorned cane hung from one of his arms.

Valerie covered her mouth with a hand and stifled a giggle as she gazed around the room. *He's just awakened a room full of female hormones.* She couldn't help but be glad - in a territorial sense - he came to meet with her. *So There!*

She consciously put a damper on the erotic sensations as they raged through her. She knew they'd never be satisfied - not if she had anything to say about it. *He's not interested, either.*

Their eyes caught, and the magician wove his way across the room to the table she'd reserved. He moved with a smooth and sexy, leisurely but steady, pace. Not a breath could be heard in the room. A metal utensil hit the floor behind the counter.

"Good afternoon, Valerie," he intoned upon his arrival at where she sat.

She'd thought to have steeled herself against him, but his seductive voice caught her by surprise. *Did he sound that way when we last spoke?* Had it been that long since she'd spoken to him? *I need to pay better attention.*

Focus, Valerie. Focus. Her stomach butterflies fluttered in the most erotic ways, and she smiled at him as he sat beside her. She slid over a few inches, which he followed. *Why does he choose to sit so close beside me instead of across from me?*

Valerie shifted and made believe she rearranged her papers and went out of her way to accommodate him. It appeared he

113

took her implied hint when he moved to sit across the table from her.

"That's a lot of paper. Is it all about the future engagements between us that we're here to talk about at this meeting?" he queried.

"Of course not," she answered as she moistened in more places than one. She wished the low timbre of his voice didn't affect her so. Had she heard a hint of enthusiasm in it?

Valerie stared at him with as little emotion as possible. "I've just come off a significant case that required a lot of study and leg work." Along with a sarcastic quirk of her brows, she added, "I do have more important business than you and your magic to attend to."

Alecksander's expression quirked. One of his hands massaged his chin. A brief flash of what could be construed as disappointment sped across his face. "Hmm."

Valerie wished she'd withheld her catty comment at her glimpse of the challenged self-esteem his sub-conscious harbored. "I like to keep the fund-raisers at a steady run.

"The Children's Services office I work for is only semi-state run. We're totally responsible for our financial burden. And the children need us."

She pulled up a file on her lap-top and pointed out her planned shows. "I like to do something on most holidays. We have regular summer events and entertainment in the city park during the fair weather months, just because."

Excitement about her work gathered and

her professional demeanor waned. "I'm sure you noticed we had a packed house for your last engagement with us, even if it was at the last minute supporters stampeded us."

He raised an eyebrow. "I noted that."

Chapter Twenty-Five

"Everybody loved your show," Valerie gushed. "That's why I asked your interest in helping us out with your superb show of magic at my, our other shows."

"And I've agreed that could be arranged."

Valerie's simmer at his usual mode of answer didn't affect her as much this time. Now came the time for the questions she'd waited so long to ask. She darted her gaze around the business they sat in.

The almost empty shop had filled since she arrived. She knew she couldn't talk to him about such personal stuff as she needed to know, in the now crowded business. Her pulse rose along with her heart's anxious pace.

Sweat moistened her brow. *How should I ask this of him?* She took a deep breath and coupled her hands. "You seem to be a man of few words. But, um, I'd like to know a bit more about you. I mean," she added quickly, "if you're going to continue to work with us on a more regular basis."

"Such as?"

Good. He's agreeable to discussion me. "Such as I need to know more about your background, etc. For legal reasons, you know."

For the first time since they met today, his eyes shaded with the distrust she recognized before, but to her relief, he reiterated, "That could be arranged."

"I'm thinking, um, that we can take a walk while we talk, to afford you some privacy." She added on a personal note as she brushed her hands past her hips, "and to burn some calories. Will that be okay with you? Do you have time?"

The darkness of the moment before left his face as he glanced around the now crowded business they sat in. "Yes. I'd like that. Do you meet with all your new entertainers on such a personal basis?" he asked with a grin as they left the building.

Valerie's face heated at his question. *No.* Not everyone she hired affected and attracted her the way he did, or had a psyche like his that spoke to her of a past trauma she needed to know about.

She couldn't tell him about the way he made her want him, but she could tell him about her abilities to connect with children, and with him. *He has psychic abilities; he'll understand.*

"Well, no, not really." *Enough on that subject.* "I guess that since I want you to level with me, it's about time that I did the same with you."

Valerie tightened her light jacket against the chilled breeze in the air. "I have empathic ability. I connect with children who are or have been abused. I *see* their problems, and am able to help them through their difficulties in life."

He bobbed his head toward her in implied understanding. "You do? That sounds interesting. Tell me, have you had this talent all your life; were you born with it?"

His immediate response sent thrills through Valerie. She could tell her confession definitely piqued an interest of his.

"Yes. Well, for most of it, anyway. I learned about my gift when I was very young. I had a girlfriend when I was about five years old. Her parents horribly mistreated and abused her.

"I saw what was going on without really being there, and it scared me that I should sense such things." She squeezed her shoulders upward in an expression of helplessness. "I was just a little thing and couldn't help her.

"No one would listen to my pleas for her safety. When she died as a result of all the wrong-doings of her parents, I vowed that I'd make them pay. But their being brought to justice for their crime never happened, as far as I know.

"As I grew up I knew I wanted to do all I could to help all the other helpless abused children of the world. I felt, maybe by helping other mistreated little ones, in some small way I could make my friend's life count.

"That's why my most recent case took all the energy and attention I have in me. It involved a little girl about the same age as my friend who died. Its similarities hit me like déjà vu. She suffered all the same traumas my friend did."

Valerie watched her arms as they whipped around in illustration of her words. She wiped a stray hair from her brow with one of her hands, lowered her arms and pulled herself together. "But I digress.

"Back to expand on my answer to your question; no. I don't take a personal interest in everyone I work with on my shows, at least not in this same way."

She stopped in their side-by-side trek on the busy city street and turned to face him. "I'm taking this opportunity and time with you because something in you has awakened my empathic ability. It wants to connect with you."

He raised an eyebrow at her. His action sent a worrisome chill through her. She wondered if she really wanted to know about that secret something in his past.

In lieu of more consideration, Valerie continued regardless of her doubts, or whether or not he wanted to say any more. She needed to explain her motives in further detail to him.

"My psychic ability for connection has plagued me since the first time I saw you. She opened her arms out to Alecksander in portrayal of her inexplicable knowledge about - and concern for - him. "I believe trauma from your past needs to be healed, and I'm the one called to do it."

His unpleasantness returned. His face blanked, and an almost visible icy barrier of wariness shot up between them.

He became like a total stranger. "Look, Lady."

Her throat bound in defense. *Lady?*

"You're wrong. I don't need any help, most certainly not from you. I don't have any problems." He sighed and the shadow on his face softened.

He took on a contrite expression. Once more he seemed changed, back to his earlier self. "I'm sorry. I really shouldn't have spoken to you so impersonally like I did."

Valerie had experienced reactions like his to her unusual ability before, but she hadn't expected it from him. She nodded in acceptance of his apology, but didn't say anything, as she'd learned to do in such circumstances.

He took up a brisk walk in silence. She trotted along to keep her step beside him. *I hope he's thinking.*

He didn't stop, but spoke to her again after a couple blocks. "It could be you're right. Maybe you can help me. Perhaps you've tapped into something. The truth of the matter is; I have no memories of a childhood."

Chapter Twenty-Six

Valerie caught up to him as often as possible during their walk. She wanted to ensure he knew he had her undivided attention while he reminisced.

"It seems I've always been here as a 'Master Magician.' There could be some trauma that happened to me at some time, but either I've chosen not to remember it, or it's being hidden from me for some reason." He wiped his brow. "I don't know."

Alecksander stopped and gazed toward Valerie. She stumbled to a stop beside him. It seemed he dove deep into her eyes when she looked up to him. For her own protection, before his past traumas absorbed too far into her psyche, Valerie's analytical side kicked in.

She returned his vision's path with one of systemic logic. "Would you like to know?"

He pulled his mouth to one side in an obvious moment of indecision. "Might as well." His pace resumed. "I'm sure my lack of knowledge has prevented any successful relationship for me. I want to love one woman and have a family, but it seems not to be."

Her chest ached as her empathic heart reached out to him. Valerie knew exactly how he felt. She wanted to reach out to him, to enfold him in her arms and let him know she was there. But she forced them to remain at her sides as his story went on.

He continued as if he bared his soul to her. "It all goes back to that possible trauma I'm unable to remember. There's a fear of being hurt. It haunts me, but I can't remember what it is."

She couldn't see his expression any longer. His walk faced straight ahead as he talked. It seemed purposeful he didn't afford her a glance of it.

"Like I've inferred, I've had a gut-reaction about you since we met."

Alecksander stopped at her words and faced her. She stiffened in uncertainty at the puzzled look he wore. "There's something about you that strongly affects me, too, but there is also something about you that tells me you will hurt me.

"It tells me that you *have* hurt me, but I can't remember any more than that. What I do know is that we can never be more than friends. I can't commit to you. Something I sense in you won't allow it."

"In me? The first time I heard your name, it too, sent iciness like death through me. But then your past reached out to me."

Alecksander continued his pace.

The healer in Valerie sought out his torment. "I've never worked with an adult, but we do seem to share a connection. Maybe we *could* see each other, um, I mean for therapy to cure you of your pain?"

She listened to herself. She'd asked to see him again. She needed to see him again. *Is this something I can handle?*

Alecksander wondered the same thing. *She wants to see me again?* His deep inside primal male instincts roared, but still something in him feared her. He reasoned if he kept himself guarded; she couldn't hurt him.

"Why do you want to help me?"

He still doesn't trust me. She shook her head and answered truthfully, "I don't know. Like I said; I've never worked with an adult before."

Alecksander arched an eyebrow and his womanizer instincts kicked in. "You want to be closer to me, don't you?"

Valerie looked away in an effort to distance herself from the egotistical man. She answered in spite of her disgust with the return of his well-known character. "Maybe."

His unfavorable nature made a sudden switch and showed her the vulnerability she'd seen before. *His mood swings like a weather-vane.*

His expression now drew her to him. "I want to be close to you, Valerie, but I can't," he admitted. "I'm drawn to be intimate with you, but it's like a forgotten memory forbids it."

Valerie sensed she could love him, too. Maybe she did love him. She wanted to tell him to give it some time. She knew she needed to give it some time, herself. *He has special powers, and I have special powers. We might be meant for each other.*

Possibilities ran through her mind like children at an Easter egg hunt. *We might have even been born for each other. Maybe we've even lived one of those past lifetimes I dream about, together.*

That could be his reason for fearing a relationship with me. Maybe I went and did something stupid in one of those past lifetimes and hurt him really badly. Not that he hadn't hurt her, in her dreams.

"We are a lot alike, you know," she said in the hope to offer some comfort to him in his baffled state of mind. Valerie continued what she wanted to say with measured calculation, "That could be the reason we're each attracted to the other."

The severity in his eyes informed her he didn't appreciate her telling him how he thought. But she couldn't stop now. "You're right; it's scary. Maybe we can take this thing one day at a time?"

"Maybe," he answered, as if from another lifetime, at least from further away than he stood. "I think our discussion is finished for now. I should go." With that, he changed direction and left her standing on the street corner of their discussion.

His constant air of aloofness both baffled and maddened Valerie. He left her before their conversation even ended. *Like it meant nothing to him at all.* His action hit her like she held no meaning to him, even though his words told her she did.

We'll be spending a lot of time together, whether he wants to or not. In time, once he gets to know me better, he'll forget his fear. Her assured view brought

a big smile to her face as she watched him
grow smaller in the distance.

Chapter Twenty-Seven

A week later ~

Alecksander stood in the Sunview Museum of Ancient History when Valerie arrived. His presence there surprised her. She'd arrived at the museum to meet with one of her volunteers, not with him. He'd not contacted her since he left her on the street.

As she spied on him from the doorway, Valerie assumed he didn't know of her arrival. He stood in front of a 12th century replica of an act of Roman Wizardry. He appeared quite intrigued, by the obvious scrutiny he indulged in.

It looked like he delved into the text in an ancient glass-encased book, as if it contained words of importance to him. He pulled out a magnifier as she watched, and examined the artifact protected behind the exhibit's see-through wall.

Valerie inhaled a deep breath for confidence and took it on herself to greet him. She hoped he'd be the friendly acquaintance she wanted him to be.

"Hello, Alecksander. I didn't expect to see you here."

His attention never left the exhibit. He responded as if to a stranger, "Hello."

Valerie gave her interest to the artifacts in the exhibition case. "These look interesting."

He didn't respond to her comment.

"What're you looking for?" she asked in an effort to begin conversation.

"History," he mumbled. His meticulous attention didn't leave the exhibit.

"What kind of history?" Valerie too, responded without a change of gaze from the book she now focused on.

"You wouldn't understand," he mumbled as he walked away from her to another part of the room's exhibit.

Well, I'm glad to see you, too.

"I'm here because I've got an appointment," she murmured in a sarcastic tone directed for his ears only. She left in the opposite direction. *Men! I only tried to make conversation.*

The next weekend-

Valerie almost dropped her phone when she answered and heard Alecksander's voice.

"Did you still want to see me again?

His offered availability to her tingled her blood through her veins, as if it ran in fast motion. "Yes," was all she managed.

"Where?"

Where? At my office? "At my office."

"I'd hoped we'd meet at a more social setting, as we did before."

Of course, you like to be eye-candy. "A more social setting?" She paused and

127

thought. "A group of my friends and I have a dinner evening planned soon. Would that be more to your liking?"

"When?"

When? "This coming Saturday."

"Where?" he asked again.

"Valentine's Lounge on East Sunview Avenue."

"The time?"

"Seven. You can invite a couple of friends if you'd like."

"It's a date."

Valerie opened her mouth and he hung up. *It's not a date!* Her blood boiled at his abrupt end to their conversation. She fisted her hand around the phone and pounded the air with it.

Saturday ~

Alecksander waited behind her door with a single red rose when she opened it to the sound of a knock. Her heart melted with his flirtatious gift. He held his arm out to her as if in offered escort.

Valerie noted he wore his trademark clothing, but remembered her lack of readiness. "I'm not quite ready, but please come in and have a seat." She backed with her door in hand and designated her living room sofa.

He raised an eyebrow.

"You are early," she reminded him.

"Of course. I'll wait."

Valerie left him and went to her bedroom.

She encountered none of his shadow as their evening out began. By his continued amorous actions, she especially thought him ready to let his guard down, not only to her, but in front of all their friends.

It didn't surprise her much when the eventuality happened and he pulled her close. She accepted the venture and prepared to be kissed by him in front of everyone. Her eyes closed and she tilted her head back, but nothing happened.

After a moment in pose, she reopened her eyes to see he hadn't moved any closer to her. Instead he'd pulled back and gazed down on her with that cursed mischievous grin of his. While her rightful anger simmered, she experienced his pain.

On any other occasion Valerie would've immediately been infuriated and humiliated. At this instance, though, her connective abilities glimpsed the same absolute misery and loneliness in his eyes as before. It mirrored out to her as if from a day gone by.

"I'm sorry if I've hurt you; I couldn't help it," he murmured, for her ears only. She looked around at their small gaggle of friends.

Clarke and his girlfriend had eyes only for each other; her co-workers chatted gaily amongst each other. They all appeared to be consciously unaware of her predicament.

A good group of actors.

At last her face grew so hot she knew it glowed; Valerie gathered up what was left of her dignity and grabbed her purse and coat. She murmured to the group, "I'm sorry. I just remembered I have to leave early," and made for the door.

129

"Valerie!" she heard Alecksander stress as he closed in on her. He caught up to her outside and held onto her arm so she would have to stop and face him. "I'm sorry. I couldn't help my atrocious behavior in there."

He glanced off into the dark horizon, and then back to her, as if he searched for his next words.

His expression appeared contrite and sincere when he again set it on her. "It was as if a power greater than my own came over me. There is no other explanation I can offer you. I should have never followed my impulse to stake," he flinched at the word.

"My claim on you in there. But that fear inside me, which we're both familiar with, wouldn't allow me to follow through with my impulse; it even now tells me that you deserved to be hurt by me."

Valerie swallowed her pride and remembered the tragedy she'd witnessed in his eyes. Yes. She did know about his problems and inabilities.

Her empathy ached for him. The misery deep within his soul portrayed itself to her every time they were together. She knew what just happened to her could have been her fault as well as his.

She took a deep breath and replied, "I'm familiar with your problem. I've seen it. I too think, for some inexplicable reason, what happened back there was just as much my fault as it was yours.

"For a like reason, from the very first time we met, I've wanted to experience a loving relationship with you,

130

as you've said you do with me. But something neither of us understands stands in our way."

She shrugged and threw her opened palms out to her sides. "We're taking this too fast. We both have trust issues which need to be worked on.

"I can't make you change; you're the only one who can do that. I can only work on myself. I suggest we do that." His expression regained its shuttered effect at her suggestion.

He's not listening. "Until you've conquered your fear of a relationship with me, there can be none." She turned her back on him and took up a quick pace down the street. *At least I live within walking distance.*

"I'll see you at SCSO's next rehearsal," she threw back over her shoulder.

****

Alecksander stood in shock that she'd turned her back on him, as he watched her retreat down the street. He cursed himself for what he'd done. *What is it in me that makes me so damned arrogant?*

He knew he'd just hurt and done a fine job of chasing away the only woman he'd ever felt he could, should and had been meant to love for eternity. *How can I make this right with her?*

He took up a slow pace and wandered gloomily down the street in the opposite direction as Valerie took. He somehow knew she'd only hurt him if he pursued her.

Chapter Twenty-Eight

Valerie tamped down any possible grudge she had with the self-absorbed man. *That's not who I am. He needs to be healed, and that is who I am - a healer of broken people.* She needed to follow her instincts now.

There are too many people in this world who've been hurt by the anger of others. It'd be best if, at least for a while, they didn't see any more of each other than absolutely necessary.

Valerie soon found her decision to abstain from seeing Alecksander any more than required, much easier to envision than enact. He filled her mind constantly. At night she dreamt about him. Her lonely nights went as such until one night he appeared at her bedside.

"Ahh!" she choked out when she awakened and he stood silhouetted in the moonlight by her bedroom window. She jerked the blankets up under her chin. "How'd you get in here?" she gasped when she caught enough breath to do so.

He said nothing. His profile didn't move. Valerie's lungs chilled at the presence she took as Alecksander's. It simply stood and watched her - in silence.

With covers in hand and wrapped around her body, she jumped out of her bed to confront him. He disappeared when she did so. She waved her arms wildly in the space he'd occupied, but they only caught thin air. She clapped her hands onto her head.

"Did I just dream that?" She stared into space, but only dark emptiness prevailed where he once stood. She scurried to the corner of her room and switched on the light. It buzzed to life. Fluorescence flooded the room and verified his absence.

Early the next morning ~

After a fitful remainder of the night's sleep - Valerie's fingers fidgeted to pick out the Master Magician's number on her cell.

She didn't want to renew conversation with him, but she needed to know why he'd entered her bedroom uninvited.

It had to have been him, in some way or another. He is a magician, after all. Did he magically cast a replica of himself into my room?

The instant he answered her call, she both demanded and chastised him at the same time, "I saw you in my bedroom last night! How dare you use your magic to insert yourself in here?"

"What are you talking about, Valerie?"

She rolled her eyes at the ceiling. His innocence sounded completely

133

sincere to her, but she wouldn't let this
one go. "Oh, come on. I saw you standing
by my window. In My Bedroom. Last night!
Don't deny this; I know how deft you are
with your skills of illusion."

"That wasn't me, Valerie. You must
believe this because I could charge you
with the same thing. You too, have been
paying visits to my bedroom at night."

"*What*?" she exclaimed. "Oh, no.
You can't accuse me of that. I
haven't paid you nightly visits." She
huffed and blurted out, "I'd never do
that. Ever! Let me ask you this; why
would I want to do that?"

Her nervous words rambled on before he
had a chance to answer her. "I've been
true to our words and have kept my
distance from you. Isn't that what we
decided on, because of your fear of my
hurting you?

"Until you have faced your demons and
solved your problem; that is the way it
must remain between us."

"All you say is irrelevant. I believe
what we've experienced is called the
'Doppelganger Effect'."

"The 'Doppel' what?"

"The Doppelganger Effect."

"Whatever in the world is that?" she
asked, unaware he drew her into
conversation with him.

"A Doppelganger is a spiritual, or
shall we say, ghostly double of someone
who is alive. Its effect is its
visitations to a living soul." He paused,
as if for addded effect to his words, then
his voice silkened with seduction, "It
visits us in our bedrooms, where we each

wish we weren't alone."

"Wonderful," Valerie sighed in resignation. "Something out there in the universe has decided that we aren't going to be able to leave each other alone even if we want to."

"Maybe," he answered, as if intrigued. "Personally, I have enjoyed your nightly visits. The way you simply stand there in the moon's sensual light. And the way you watch me with your beautiful, intoxicating hazel eyes," he stated with his normal smooth and sexy tone.

Valerie breathed easier. The side of him she treasured soothed her troubled soul.

"Will that be all?" he abruptly asked.

The comfort of her moment shattered. His wall had gone up again.

"No," she murmured. "I mean, Yes!" she quickly corrected.

"Then good day," he said and clicked his phone off.

"Good Day," she echoed into her dead phone, which she then threw against the wall. The cell phone broke into two pieces and clattered onto the floor.

Valerie burnt at his moodiness. She'd never lost her temper and become physically angry with anyone, but Alecksander and his split second changes of personality. *And now I've got to go to work.*

Valerie showered and prepared herself a cup of tea. She hoped the hot drink would complement the soothing shower and further relax her before she began another day.

Later that morning ~

Her supervisor almost jumped on her, as if she lay in wait; the moment Valerie showed her face through SCSO's doorway. "I'm so happy to see you here early, Valerie!"

Valerie sucked in a short breath. *What's happened now?* Her morning tea hadn't produced the desired effect, and she could tell by the sound of Sandy's voice today's events would do little to settle her nerves.

She paused and uttered a wary reply, "Good morning, Sandy." Her gaze met her supervisor's before she broke contact and continued on to her desk. "I don't usually receive such a greeting from you on the start of a new day. What's happened?"

Sandy trailed her and plopped a heavy file of paperwork she held, onto Valerie's desk.

We've been notified of a possible mistrial on a previous case of yours."

Chapter Twenty-Nine

Valerie stared at the documentation on her desk and realized she recognized it. Her insides knotted. *We placed this child over a year ago.* She picked the pages up and shuffled through them.

Surely there must be some kind of limitations, which has run out. She stared up at her supervisor and partially spoke her thoughts, "This case finished over a year ago."

"I know," her frustrated supervisor responded. "Some beaurocratic mistake somewhere; I'm sure. I know you can take care of it," she stated as she left for her own office.

Valerie's busy day began with the record's section of the court. She followed-up with conversations with the attorneys involved in the questioned case. Her involved interactions kept her irritation with Alecksander's personality quirks at bay.

Valerie's frustration with the magician went overlooked when she arrived at that night's rehearsal for SCSO's fundraiser. The Master Magician's seductive punctual appearance there, after her ahead-of-time arrival, kept the rebirth of her anger with him at bay.

The magnetic air of self-importance embodied in his presence enveloped everyone in the auditorium when Alecksander made his bold entrance onto the stage. Valerie's eyes locked onto him. She swallowed her breath. Her thoughts cleared.

She couldn't even remember when Alecksander first entered the auditorium. Her bodily sensations only knew he stood there in front of her - now. She shook herself back to her senses and owned her professionalism.

With her identity intact, Valerie ascended the stage steps, where she held one of her hands out to greet him. "Hello, Alecksander." She raised her wristwatch to meet her glance. "Exactly on time."

Alecksander raised an eyebrow to her. Indubitably. Shall we begin?"

"Oh, yes! Of course." Her face heated. The seductive warmth of his proximity filled Valerie with other entirely different thoughts.

She reprimanded and gave herself a quick reminder of their purpose there for the evening. *What is wrong with me? The man is an ass. You should be ashamed of yourself, Miss Baldwin. We've got work to do.*

She returned to her seat beside Sandy. They sat in the front-row center seats of the house to watch the final rehearsal of the magician's performance. Valerie believed he needed no more practice. His show seemed already perfected.

"Good Evening, Ladies and Gentlemen," Alecksander improvised. His words echoed back to them from all sides of the almost empty auditorium. He bowed in front of his imagined audience.

Regardless of the ownership of her chosen line of work, Valerie didn't feel at all like her professional self by the end of the magician's final "dress rehearsal." Her body lightened. It seemed she'd float away.

Weepy excitement overcame her and she wiped her eyes. Her airways tickled with each breath she inhaled. It again seemed to her she acted like a school-girl with a crush. No other choice remained open - her heart led the way.

Valerie sat with her elbows on her knees and her hands clasped under her chin. Alecksander's presence captivated her. Although, his effect on her changed after each show, just as it did tonight.

At the end of the rehearsal, the magician gathered the props of his stage presence without a sound. He left the building in the same silence as he came, without as much as a bye and bye to Valerie or anyone.

His method of departure always stunned the two women. "Well, of course, he knows we need him for his skills, which are beyond compare," Sandy grumbled to Valerie as he vanished from their presence.

Valerie alerted to attention and snapped out of her reverie at Sandy's words. Memories of the times he'd hurt her returned. "I'm surprised he can get through doors with that *ego* of his. He has annoyed me since the day I first met him."

"But in your heart, you still nurse a warm spot for him; don't you, Valerie?"

I'm not that obvious, am I? "The man's an arrogant anal opening. How do you know if I ever *did* have a 'warm spot for him, anyway?"

Sandy chuckled. "You put on a good show when you berated him about his 'ego', but it didn't work, trust me. You think I don't notice the way you sit on the edge of your seat while he rehearses?"

The stuffiness of the room's temperature suffocated Valerie. She fought for a breath and ducked her head so Sandy wouldn't notice the warmth on her face. She gathered her purse and jacket up with fumble-fingers and readied to leave.

"It really isn't what you think." she mumbled. "I need to get home now. I'll see you in the morning." Valerie stuffed her belongings under an arm and left without even a backward glance at her supervisor.

She couldn't bear her embarrassment when she arrived at home that evening. *I can't imagine what I must look like to Sandy at his rehearsals. That man is nothing but trouble. I'm going to bed and forget tonight ever happened.*

As she undressed for bed, the corner of her eye caught the area where the Doppelganger made itself known to her each night. A full glance to her window revealed nothing stood there, yet, but Valerie clenched her nightwear in her fists

140

and stomped out of the bedroom for the privacy of her bathroom.

She banged the door into its frame behind her. Thoughts of how she allowed that man to affect her made her crazy. *It's me! He wouldn't be able to exercise such control over me if I didn't allow him to.* She slammed a bar of soap onto the shower's corner counter and engaged in her night's bathing ritual.

After her shower, Valerie slipped into her nighttime lingerie and threw herself onto her bed. Her heart ached with the ageless longing, which beset her evenings. *Why must I always be alone?*

She tried to empty her mind and sleep, but couldn't keep Alecksander out of it. It seems we already know each other, and that we're getting so close – but to what? She imagined she witnessed the same knowledge in his eyes, too.

Valerie buried her face in the mattress – where the unknowns of her situation continued their torment of her. Why couldn't he believe she'd never hurt him. There had to be some other reason, one he wouldn't betray to her.

Chapter Thirty

Next morning ~

Valerie sat up on her bed. Her reflection reflected back to her from the mirror on the wall opposite. She gripped her fingers onto the sides of her head. *Why is my perception lacking?*

It seemed certain to her she knew the grounds for her problem with Alecksander. *He's told me he will never form a relationship with me. But he leaves it at that!* "Why won't he just tell me the truth!" she cried out to her reflection.

It would ease my soul in so many ways. Because of him, for the first time in her history with the children's fund-raisers, Valerie didn't look forward to her organization's rehearsals. "And there's another rehearsal tomorrow night," she groaned.

Valerie and Sandy, along with the other SCSO membership who were present for the night's rehearsal, broke into a round of applause when Alecksander bowed at the end of his evening's practice performance.

"I'm shocked!" Sandy confided in an aside to Valerie. "The man has actually waited here long enough to hear his applause."

Though her hormones gave Valerie a pleasurable sensation he remained, she withheld her happiness when she whispered back, "I am, too."

"I'll bet you are," came Sandy's sarcastic reply.

Valerie gave her friend the "look," but chose not to justify the comment Sandy tossed at her, with any follow-up.

"Look. He's coming our way," Sandy pointed out to her.

Valerie fought not to jump up when she and Sandy stood to acknowledge Alecksander's approach. *Why must I always feel I've discovered and must hold onto someone dear to my heart when he's around? This is so not like me. The man's making me crazy.*

The magician gripped his trademark cane in both fists before him when he arrived at their sides. "Good evening, Ladies. I know I've never taken the time, as I should have, to discuss this with you.

"I'm sorry for that, but I've chosen to wait until my performance is perfected before I listen to my employer's opinion of it."

Valerie couldn't believe what she assumed she heard. *The Great Alecksander has a fear of rejection?*

When he first looked into Sandy's eyes - instead of hers - a sharp pang of jealousy knotted in Valerie's chest. "What did you think of my performance?" he

143

asked.

Sandy clapped her hands together in front of her chest. She held them there as if in prayer mode.

"I think your show is marvelous!" she gushed. "It needs no 'perfection'. I've thought that from your very first rehearsal.

"We're so fortunate to have Alecksander Stone, The Great Master Magician, perform for our small show!" She drew Valerie to her and squeezed in a side-hug. "We are indebted to Valerie for acquiring your services for us."

She exchanged her perspective from one face to the other. "Now I believe you two might still have some paperwork and last minute discussion about several minor details to finish up with."

Valerie nodded in recollection, though she didn't look forward to the torture of him alone with her.   "Yes. There's still one final signature of committal we need."

Alecksander laid his molten gaze upon her. "I'll do anything you want, Valerie. We can do it tonight, if you'd like."

The wink and suggestive tone of voice he used melted Valerie's insides. Her heart raced. *Oh please, don't let my face blush right now.* Her plea did no good as her face heated to the same temperature as the rest of her body.

She sought out her friend's face for support. The knowledgeable grin on Sandy's face confirmed Valerie's plight.
"All the necessary paperwork is right up there in your office, isn't it, Valerie?" Sandy asked as she designated the

upstairs.

Valerie moved her head in the negative as she thought about where the "necessary paperwork," rested. It sat in a small stack of administrative correspondence on her dining room table.

She picked up her purse, ventured to look Alecksander in the eye, and gave a toss of her head toward the upstairs offices. "It's somewhere else. I'll meet you in my office upstairs, in um," she glanced at her wristwatch and continued, "Say half an hour?"

"Why not right now?" he countered.

Her spine stiffened. "Because I need to run home and pick up the work you need to sign. It won't take me long."

Sandy tilted her head at Valerie, as if in question.

Valerie stared at her. "It's there because I was ironing out those last minute details you mentioned this morning," she supplied without waiting for Sandy to formulate the question.

"I can go with you there. No need for you to bother with an unnecessary trip."

Sandy clapped the magician on the back. "That sounds like an excellent idea! What do you think, Valerie?"

"Um, yeah," she murmured as she made her way to the exit door.

Alecksander caught up to Valerie in the parking lot. Her keys jangled as she played with them in her hand. *I don't want to drive out there in the same car.* "You can follow me," she instructed.

"My intentions. I wouldn't want to be stuck at your place without my car when

I'm ready to leave."

Of course he wouldn't want to be stuck *at my place.* *He obviously has different reasons for not wanting to drive out with me.* "My condo complex has a secured parking garage.

She eased into her car and put down the window. "You should be able to find a place to park on the street beside it."

He nodded and turned toward his car.

Chapter Thirty-One

Valerie broke into giggles on her drive home. *I've got no need to tell him where he can and cannot park.* He could no doubt park anywhere he wanted to. *Of course he'll be able to find a place to park.*

She pulled her jacket on when she stepped out of her little car, but she didn't need it. Her pulse warmed her in the most delightful ways. When she walked out of the parking garage, she saw Alecksander already stood at the building's arched entryway.

As always, his presence commanded her awe. *He embellishes the property.* Her pace sped up as she approached - until she realized she didn't want to appear too eager to be at his side. *He doesn't want to be "stuck" here, remember?*

"This shouldn't take us too long," she said without greeting as she breezed past him. She heard Alecksander followed as if just a step behind her. In the foyer of her home, Valerie gestured to her living room.

"You wait in there. I'll get the paper you need to sign and then you'll be able to leave." *Without being stuck here since you have your own car with you.* When Alecksander attempted to follow, she shooed him back into the living room.

It only took her a moment to grab the necessary paper off her dining table. She snatched a pen from a counter she passed and rejoined him in the living room. He moved over on the sofa he sat on and glanced down to the vacated spot at his side.

Valerie at first balked, but then reconsidered. *I can sit there. It'll be easier to point out the specifics on this paper he'll sign.* She spread the documentation out onto the coffee-table before him, and lowered herself to sit at his side.

"This is what I need you to sign." She glanced up at him from the paper on the table. "You'll want to read this first."
The corners of his mouth lifted up in a smile her quivering insides found little resistance to. But she stayed firm in her resolve.

"You think I don't trust you?" He accepted the pen from her and signed his name on the specified space, without reading a word he signed his agreement to. The pen flew up with a flourish as he finished. "I don't need to read it."

Valerie lifted the signed paper in her hand, and rose to take it back to her briefcase in her room. "You can leave now," she tossed back as she left him where he sat.

His voice followed her. "I can?" he questioned after she stood in her room.

She stopped in motion. The paper wafted onto her bed. Her heart danced in an energetic tap-dance. Tickles flowed through her. *You must.* When she turned, her eyes met his while he stood in the room's doorway.

He followed me anyway. "Is there anything else I can do for you?" Tell-tale warmth spread over her face. *No. Not that.*

"Um, I mean do you have any further requirements that need to be taken care of?" *Darn it!* "I meant, about the show you have planned for us. Is there anything else I can do for you about *that*?"

"It seems too long since we've had any real time together, alone," Alecksander confessed in a moment of truth they both experienced. The distance between them decreased with their like steps. They soon stood face-to-face.

He whispered to her, "It could be I've waited my whole lifetime for you." His breath landed on her neckline as he nuzzled his lips to it, then nibbled on one of her earlobes.

His action stirred what seemed an ageless passion within her. "Longer than a lifetime," she whispered in the commitment of the eternal devotion she experienced.

He helped her out of her suit jacket and she loosened his shirt. Their long-awaited loving increased as he helped her out of the rest of her clothing and they inched their way to her bed. She lay down with pleasure and brought him with her.

Finally, this would be it. *The end to my hormonal torture.* Her femininity throbbed for him and she reached down to help him remove the remainder of his clothing, but one of his hands caught hers and he moved it away.

She lay there in total shock as he pulled completely away from her and redressed himself. Their moment together ended the same way as she recalled his public kiss and most of his rehearsals had.

So this is it. There he was dressed and ready to leave her as if nothing just happened between them. Her whole body burned with embarrassment and anger with the thought of the situation she found herself in.

Is he afraid of my rejection? "What's wrong? Where are you going?" she asked.

His whole manner and tone of voice changed, "Nothing's wrong. I've enjoyed our visit, but we can't do this. Now I've got to get back to my office."

Her anger at last flared at him, though it still emerged against her will. She sat up with a stiffened back and stared daggers through Alecksander. "No. Oh, no you don't.

"You've toyed with me long enough. I, too, sense I've waited what seems all my life for you. I also sense the knowledge I have is the same as you say you have about me."

She pounded one of her fists into the mattress at her side. "I won't allow you to torture us in this way any longer. You, kind sir," she indicated with a strong finger pointed in his direction. "You have

150

a problem for which you need professional help."

Instead of ownership and acceptance of his fault, he informed her, "No. I have no problem. I've just realized I can't allow myself to become involved in a relationship with an employer. It's been that way from the beginning."

As if that should account for his atrocious behavior! "It has *not* been that way 'from the beginning'! You've certainly had no problem with all your teasing up to this point! Look at me.

"Just look at me!" She gestured with one of her hands as it flowed in illustration over her unclad body on the bed. Look at the embarrassing position you've put me in!"

Alecksander reached for the door and as he closed it behind him, his muffled words came her way, "You should get dressed."

Chapter Thirty-Two

Valerie thought her head would burst into flames with irritation at his nonchalance. "And you should get out of my life and stay away from me!" she screamed as she threw her medieval-styled bedside lamp toward the door.

She gasped at what she'd done in retaliation and remembered his supposed reason for being there. *Did he sign it?* Valerie sent her hateful vision to the closed door. She didn't care whether or not he'd authorized the paper on her coffee table.

It would take some work, but she knew other entertainment for SCSO's upcoming fund-raisers could be found. "I never want to see you again!" she screamed. Her head throbbed with the force of her voice.

She returned her attention to the ancient shattered lamp on the floor. *What have I done?* Tears came to her eyes. Her beautiful and treasured antique lamp he'd bought for her at the annual Re-enactor's Faire lay scattered about in shatters.

Valerie broke into tears at her act

of anger, stuffed her face into her pillow, and pounded on the mattress beside her. Through muffled screams she exclaimed, "I hate him! I hate him! I hate him!" until they changed to quiet little words of, "I love him," and she drifted off into a fitful slumber.

Her head still ached when Valerie re-awoke in a bad temperament, still early that morning. She credited it to the destructive way she allowed herself to respond to Alecksander and his loathsome characteristics.

By her loss of control, she'd not only hurt Alecksander the way she meant to, but she'd also hurt herself by her rejection of him. She remembered her habit of never any lost moments of temper with the children she cared for.

The little ones she worked with had problems, but their troubles weren't hers. They didn't choose their circumstances. Her temper always held even, but not with Alecksander. She couldn't even reconcile it with his adulthood.

I never lose my temper. Why'd I lose it with him? He needs healing. After she answered her own question, Valerie engaged in self-counsel, "I didn't handle that like I should've."

Her fit of anger with him struck her as familiar, but she couldn't drag the elusive memory out. She took a deep breath and straightened her posture. "I'm a professional woman," she reminded herself, "and I handle myself with facts, not fantasy."

I've got to free myself of any

emotional involvement. It's now up to him. He must learn to deal with his past and the reason behind his fears. She knew he'd never be able to love anyone if he didn't do that and regain his ability to trust.

Maybe it's best this way, if we don't see each other again. Until he seeks counseling and regains his ability to trust, he will never be able to release those emotions I crave from him. She hoped he would.

Her telephone rang later on the same morning, Saturday. Valerie groaned as she rolled over to retrieve her cell phone from her bedside. Today was her day to sleep in and she'd not rested well during the night after Alecksander's departure.

She moaned. "What time is it?" A groan escaped her when she looked to her clock and saw the time sat at eight a.m. *Who could be calling at this hour on a Saturday?* "Hello?"

"Good morning, Valerie," Alecksander's smooth low tone soothed. Her anger of the previous night ebbed with the sexy timbre of his unexpected voice. The sound of it intoxicated her half-conscious senses.

Excitement bubbled in her lower stomach and further areas. In an instant she bolted upright in a state of full wakefulness. Traitorous thrills shot up through her body, but she kept her composure. "Oh. Hello."

"I'm calling to tell you how sorry I am I made you so angry with me yesterday."

"No. It's I who should be sorry for

losing my temper the way I did. That wasn't like me at all."

"No," he copied. "I should never have led you on; the way I did. And I shouldn't have left you the way I did, either. I hope you're not still angry with me."

She had to end this merry-go-round of blame acceptance. "Trust me, Alecksander; I'm no longer angry. Neither have I rejected you, but I still believe you need counseling before we can go any further in our relationship; if that's what we have."

"You're a counselor. Will you do it for me?"

"That I cannot do. You know I work with children, who we both know well that you are not," she answered while visions of his toned and sexy body stimulated her senses and began the erotic ebbs and flows anew.

"I wish I could work with you, but you need to see someone who is trained in working with adult relationships. You need to visit someone who can help you learn to trust and give to another adult in a loving and caring fashion.

"You say you don't know why you're unable to commit and give yourself to another. And that you don't remember much from your past. If that's the case, you might even want to check with a past-life regression therapist.

"That person will be able to take you back to the memories of your childhood that you've hidden from yourself."

His defensive tone returned, "I don't believe I need to go that far. There isn't anything wrong with me. I don't have any 'head' problems."

I'm sure you don't. She refrained from allowing her moment of sarcasm to sound in her voice. "But as a counselor, myself, that's the only remedy I see for your future, for our future, if there will be any," she calmly asserted.

His tone softened. "If that's so, I wish you would please think about taking the job. You're the only one who understands me."

Valerie remained firm. "No. I won't. I can't. It would be unethical, to say the very least. Hold onto your phone for a second and I'll find you a list of reputable therapists that I have here."

She placed her phone on her bed and fired up her computer to print out her list of names, then picked up her phone again. "You still there?" she asked, not sure if he'd hung around long enough to get the names from her.

"Yes. I'm still here," came his dry reply.

The crisp sound of fresh computer paper crinkled between Valerie's fingers. "I have two lists here for you. I'll read them to you now, and you may pick them up from me at any time."

"What kind of counselors are they? I refuse to see a children's counselor."

"If you'll remember, I don't plan to send you to one. The list of names I have here are relationship counselors and regression therapists. The relationship counselors I'd recommend are. . ."

Chapter Thirty-Three

Alecksander sighed after the fifth name she read. "How long are these lists?"

"Not too," Valerie replied between names. She paused and added, "The list of regression therapists I have for you is even shorter. There aren't too many of those in practice, yet."

"Why don't you just email them to me?"

Of course he didn't want to see her and retrieve them in person. "I can do that."

"We'll talk more about this later," he squeezed in as he hung up his end of the conversation.

Well, that was abrupt, but I guess that's his way. She hoped he cared enough to have taken her seriously about his need to be counseled. *We'll just have to wait and see what happens.*

★★★★

Alecksander jabbed the disconnect button on his phone. He remained the master, always in control of any friendships he began - that way no one ever hurt him. The muscles inside his neck ground together.

He remained sure he'd made inference of him and Valerie getting back together, and that they should spend more time with each other, and she'd rejected his offer with stipulations.

Women didn't refuse him. *No woman does that.* But this one had. That made her different than most. It also gave her the capability of hurting him. But *she's out of my life now.*

He possessed no intention of making contact with her suggested list of therapists. If he never followed through, he'd never have to worry about her ability to hurt him.

Yet his psyche wouldn't allow his rest. He couldn't escape the list of names she'd emailed him. They intrigued him beyond reason. He dreamed about them. They tormented him without remorse.

Alecksander's mystical orb of answers wouldn't even assist him. He spent many hours seated in front of it, but each session ended in mental debate. His forehead throbbed in his palms.

After much inner struggle, he gave in to what seemed inevitable. *There might just be something to this crazy idea of Valerie's.* All the questions about his past he had no memories of plagued him.

Alecksander first visited with a relationship counselor and explained his difficulties to her. After little progress, she recommended a more experienced regression therapist whom she believed he should see.

"You first need to confront your lost memories before we can work on your current

relationship abilities. I have the name
of a qualified regression therapist I can
refer you to," she told him as she surfed
through the files on her computer system.

Alecksander accepted the name and
number she gave him. He returned to his
home without even a glance at Valerie's
list of recommended regression therapists,
and dialed the number given to him – Dr.
Samuel Bower.

****

Valerie stared at her cell phone.
She ached inside at the way Alecksander
hung up on her. *He's a proud man, too much
pride for his own good.*

She didn't think he'd seriously
consider her suggestion to seek out one of
her recommended counselors. If he didn't,
then that would have to be accepted. She
swallowed her emotions. *I can deal with
it.*

She knew their relationship couldn't
go any further if he couldn't, or didn't,
trust her with his emotions. If he cared
so little about their situation he wouldn't
make an effort, then there could be no
place in her life for him.

But a piece of her still held out
hope. *Maybe he will seek counseling and
he'll change. Maybe one day in some far
off future we will meet again, and maybe
then we can build a relationship.*

Valerie began her day the same as she
had for years. Day off or not, she dressed
and went to her office. Off days enabled
her to surf the files in search of a
forgotten child, without the interruption
of phone calls and new assignments.

She flipped through the windows on her

computer until her head jerked and her eyes glued to a picture as she scanned. The mental stumble jerked her to attention.

The picture plucked her heart strings. Her emotions arched in recognition. "That boy, I remember him," she mumbled to the empty office she sat in. He wore the same rags as on the day she remembered. "He's the little waif I met on the bus!"

Her muscles tensed and surged to jump out of her chair. She tingled with excitement. Thrills gathered in her chest at her sight of his picture. *Maybe now I'll be able to find him again.*

Valerie traced one of her index fingers down the computer screen's text. "He's an abandoned street child," She mumbled. The screen smudged as she ran her finger over it, but found no further information. *Where is he now?*

She grabbed her purse and headed for the streets. Outside her office building she stopped and stared back and forth. *Guess I'll check where I first saw him.* No luck came with her targeted bus terminal, so she hopped a bus and checked another.

On a mission after she didn't find him at the second terminal, Valerie walked the streets of Sunview in random. As was her way, she forgot all about her own problems when faced with those of a child's.

Valerie soon happened onto an unsavory part of town, on the cusp of a small crowd of street people. They gathered in a circle; their interests centered on something. She sidled in closer to see what held their rapt attention.

Her spirits rose when she saw the little boy she searched for, in the group's center. He worked deftly with a deck of cards. Some paraphernalia like she'd seen at Alecksander's shop, rested by his side.

Supplies at the boy's side all appeared old and well used. A few even appeared broken. A plastic cup about the size of a gallon jug, with its top cut off, sat on his other side. The people in observance of his activities placed coins in it.

She watched until he indicated his show ended and stood to bow. His audience applauded and left. The people's murmured conversation lingered in the air after them.

Valerie stepped forward and cleared her throat to gain his attention after the last straggler left.

The boy popped his innocent vision up at her. "Yes, ma'am?" He did his best to act like he didn't recognize her, but the alarm in his widened eyes told her he did. She smiled and he let a small amount of breath out.

"Are you mad at me?"

Chapter Thirty-Four

She shook her head.

The rest of his breath came out. "I thought you were gonna be real mad at me."

"What's past is past." She knelt down to his level and indicated his array of magical appliances. "You seem to be quite an entrepreneur."

He skewed his little eyebrows. "An entre . . . what?"

"Someone who runs his own business."

He straightened and puffed his chest out. "I am."

"Is yours successful?"

He cocked his head and Valerie took his inquisitive expression as an indication she should rephrase her question. "Do you make much money?"

His posture surged. "Oh, yeah! I make a whole bunch!" he exclaimed as he jostled his plastic cup. Coins overflowed from his make-do bank.

He stooped to scoop up the few fallen coins and placed them on the top of the copper and silver heap. A few green notes peeked out from the masses of metal. "I can buy some food with this!"

His excited statement alarmed the social worker in Valerie. "Where's your home?"

He poked his arm off to his side and pointed.

Valerie frowned and the children's care-giver in her spoke, "Don't you think you're a little young to be out on the streets alone, supporting yourself?"

He gave her an impish little grin. "No. I'm used to it. I done take care of myself all my life." He thumped one of his thumbs on his chest as if in pride. "I'm a big boy; almost a man."

His declaration plucked an elusive memory in Valerie. "Hmm," she acknowledged. "I've stood a little further back," she gestured with her arm to where she'd stood, "in the crowd you gathered with your trade, and watched you.

"You appear to be a very accomplished little magician. Where'd you learn your magic? Have you worked at this for long?"

"I don't remember. I've just been able to do stuff like this all my life."

Her heart caught. *Alecksander used almost the same words about his skills.* "All your life?" She winked at him. "Come on, you had to have learned it somewhere."

He focused his still wide eyes on her face and gave his head a violent shake. His wavy blond locks flew like wheat stalks in a storm.

"Think," Valerie implored. *Remember.*

He stomped a foot. "I don't want to. You won't like me any more if I do."

Valerie smiled and gave her head a

163

compassionate shake. "Now why would you think that, honey?"

That's why my momma didn't like me. She said I scared her and to go away and leave her alone."

What? "She kicked you out? How old were you?" Valerie scowled and took a quick glance at the city buildings around them. "Where is she now?" she menaced.

The boy shrugged as if he didn't care. "I dunno."

Valerie gentled her voice, "But who takes care of you, honey?"

"I told you! I take care of myself."

"But you're too little for that."

"Says, who?" The little boy stomped one of his feet along with his demand.

His insistence took Valerie aback. "Well, I do, for one," she ventured without condemnation.

His foot stomped again as he stressed, "Don't worry about me. I'm not 'too little'! I told you I'm a big boy - almost a man. I've taken care of myself all my life."

"But who took care of you when you were a baby?'

"I don't remember when I was that little."

A breath of a chuckle escaped Valerie. "Of course you don't. None of us do. What's your name?"

He returned his attention to the paraphernalia he gathered up before he answered. "Scotty." He looked up to her. "What's yours?"

"Valerie." She offered a hand for him to shake. After which, she jumped into action in order to catch him off guard.

She knew no one would miss him since he'd already received the label of "Street Child."

"Let's collect all your stuff and leave this place." Together they stuffed all of his belongings into his tattered duffle-bag.

"Where're we going?" he asked after they finished.

"You don't have to take care of yourself any longer. I'm going to see that you're taken care of from now on." She hefted his bag onto her back and clasped one of his cold little hands into her warmer one.

"But where are we going?" he reiterated as she led him down the street.

Valerie gave his hand a gentle squeeze. "I'm taking you with me to my home tonight. On Monday I'm going to find you a good home of your own.

At Valerie's condo ~

Scotty threw off his raggedy coat at Valerie's condo. He looked around himself and exclaimed, "Hey! This is a nice home you have!" He wrapped his arms about his shoulders and shivered off the cold.

"It's so warm here." He bounced onto and disappeared into her over-stuffed chair. His voice sounded from somewhere within its plush folds, "This is so comfortable. It kinda feels like a soft pile of warm mushy mud in the summer."

A 'pile of warm mushy mud'? "When were you in a 'pile of warm mushy mud'?" *It must be someplace he's played.* "Is that someplace you've played?"

Too busy with his marvels over her home, Scotty didn't look to her when he answered. "Sometimes."

"Where is it?"

His little voice filled with excitement. "There's a pile of mud at this place they call a 'dump'. I play there in the summertime." The enthusiasm left his voice as if he didn't like what he had to say next. "I've slept there, too."

"Oh, Honey," Valerie moaned. "Have you slept in that horrible place often?"

"Only when my momma first dropped me off there. Then I met some nice people getting food from the cans there and they told me I could go stay with them at the church. Are you going to take me back to be with them tomorrow?"

"No," Valerie drawled. *Not if I can help it.* "But I would like to take you to work with me to talk to some important people on Monday."

Scotty's face froze into the same expression Valerie remembered from when he first thought her mad at him. "Are they big scary people?"

She smiled and hugged him. "No. They're nice people. They like to help children like you."

"Are they like the nice people at the dump?"

Valerie smiled and breathed another quiet laugh at his innocence. The 'nice' people she worked with weren't homeless, like the people she assumed Scotty spoke of at the dump, but she guessed they were the same in that they were nice people.

"Well, yes, I suppose they are."

"Are they like you?" he asked.

"Yes, like me."

Scotty's expression lost its fear at her confirmation. "Good. What're we going to talk to them about?"

Chapter Thirty-Five

Valerie clapped her hands onto the boy's skinny shoulders. "We're going to talk to them about finding a good home for you."

"But I thought I could live here with you."

Her heart tugged the same way it did with each child she placed. "Would you like that?"

"Yes. You're a nice lady." He looked around himself and then back to her. "And your home is warm and clean."

Valerie ached at the improbability of his request. "Well, that might be arranged - for a while, anyway. But wouldn't you like to live in a home with both a mommy and a daddy? That's what they will want to find for you."

The little face in front of her frowned, and Valerie infused herself with excitement and clapped her hands together. "But maybe you can stay here with me in the meantime!"

"No!" He stomped his foot. "I want to stay here with you forever. I don't want another momma. Momma's are mean!"

Valerie hugged him to her. "Not all mommas are 'mean', honey."

His little face scowled with obvious meaning. "My momma was mean. She didn't like me."

Valerie frowned. "Oh. I'm so sorry, honey. What about your daddy? Was he mean?"

Scotty shrugged. "I dunno. I've never had a 'daddy'. I don't know if they're mean, too. What I want is to stay here with you. You're not like a momma. You're nice."

She kept her hold on him tight. "Don't you worry, honey. I'll make sure you have a good home. It'll be one you like; I promise." Valerie knew she'd love to take Scotty under her care; the fact she couldn't left her bereft.

"Have you eaten dinner yet?"

He shook his head. "Nope."

"Well, we'll fix that,"

"Hey! Where'd you go?" he clamored after her when she left him alone.

"I'm in the kitchen. Come on in; I thought you'd follow me when I left."

"I didn't know if it'd be all right," Scotty called.

The patter of his feet echoed on the polished hardwood floor in her condo as he ran in the direction she'd taken. He soon joined her in the kitchen.

Valerie already had some cabinets opened and considered her food-stores when he reached her side.

"Hey! You have lots of food! I've never seen so much food in one place in my life!"

I've never thought about that before.
She turned and smiled at him. "What would you like to eat?"

"Can I have anything I want?"

"Well, most anything, anything I have, that is."

Scotty's little eyes lit up. "I know! S'prise me!"

She raised her eyebrows at him, with wonders of what a child like him would like. "Are you sure?"

"Yeah! You prob'ly have a lot of good food here!"

"Okee-dokee," she breathed. "Would you like to watch some television while I prepare your dinner?"

"Wow! You have a Television?" he marveled. "Did it come from one of those big windows where you can watch it from the street?"

Valerie paused and went over that in her mind for a minute. *It probably did.* She took one of his hands and escorted him to a seat in front of her TV, then picked up her remote and turned the screen on.

Scotty did a double take. "Wow! How'd you do that? You didn't even touch it!"

Valerie lifted her hand toward him in illustration.

He jumped back up. "Wow! That's like magic! We both do magic!"

Not really. "What do you like to watch on television?"

"I can have my choice?"

"Yes you can."

"I've never had my choice before. Somebody behind the big window decided that for me."

170

"Do you like to watch cartoons?"
Valerie asked as she tapped in the Cartoon
Network's call numbers on the remote.

She knew she'd picked a winner when
she watched Scotty's eyes light up at the
antics of animated characters on her color
3-D television screen.

"Wow! It's like they're right here!"
He plopped down cross-legged onto the
floor in front of her entertainment center.

Scotty's boyish delight warmed
Valerie's soul as she left him for the
kitchen to prepare some dinner for them.

"Dinner's ready!" she called out from
the kitchen about a half-hour later.

Scotty ran in and when he saw the
prepared dish he showered her with his
amazement again, "Wow! Little hot dogs and
curved pipe stuff!"

"It's called "Weenie Mac," Valerie
stated and placed a filled bowl on her
table in front of him.

He scooted into a chair in front of
the bowl and scooped up a mouthful with
the spoon at its side. "I luff it!" he
mumbled through the food in his mouth.

After dinner Scotty gave Valerie
another surprise. When she finished with
the dinner dishes and joined him in the
Den, he presented all his magic show
paraphernalia, which he'd unpacked while
she cleaned up after them.

Just like a seasoned showman, he
motioned for her to be seated and prepared
to give her a private show of his magical
skills.

Thoughts about Alecksander hadn't

spent much time in her mind after she found her little street urchin again. The boy's magic show smacked her full force with memories of The Master Magician.

A lump formed in her chest. *I wonder where he is. Has he done anything about his problems?*

Chapter Thirty-Six

Who am I?

After the first counselor Alecksander called directed him to a regression therapist; he proceeded to visit the said counselor. The six months of regression visits he settled in for, promised the full hypnotic journey into his past.

At their first session of hypnosis, his therapist guided Alecksander back as far as his childhood. There, the magician recognized he'd indeed been a child at some point in time. After his session, he emerged refreshed. "I was really there. I saw myself as a child!" he blurted out to the counselor.

His therapist smiled and relaxed into his leather-backed chair. "Good! Search your emotions of that time, if you can. Did you see anything there that might've caused your current relationship problems?"

Alecksander closed his eyes and searched his memory of the time he just visited. "Not that I can see." He reopened his eyes and stared at his therapist, "I'm not really sure I saw anything of importance, while regressed there."

"Nothing? Could you have experienced any traumas while there, perhaps?" the doctor seeded for the growth of Alecksander's recollections.

"No. I don't remember anything like that."

His therapist put his hands to his temples, as if in deep thought. "then it seems our answer must lie in a previous lifetime."

Alecksander stared at him in disbelief. "You really think I've lived before?"

"Isn't that why you're here?"

Alecksander nodded; still not sure if he believed it.

The therapist continued as if there'd not been a break in his words. "Now that we've found your childhood self, we can dig deeper to that past life, confront it, and heal it."

Alecksander clapped his hands onto his lap with a loud slap and girded himself with a stretch of his arms. "I'm ready when you are."

The therapist glanced at his office's standard wall clock. "Time remains for a double session with you today. Shall we begin?"

A light-headed euphoria, one not experienced on the trip to his childhood, invaded Alecksander's mind while he listened to his therapist's coached words. Instinct for self-survival gripped and urged him to fight his way back to the present.

His impulse eventually succumbed and Alecksander released his grasp on reality as he knew it. He saw himself and an old man who taught him to perform magic. The grizzled being whipped him when he didn't perform his supernatural spells correctly.

The pain yanked Alecksander from observer to participant. He learned how to make himself appear and disappear, how to present fair ladies with flowers, and other feats of legerdemain.

When he perfected his skills at those things, his mentor forced him to do bad things with his magic. He learned to spook horses and cause their riders to fall into deep waters. With the heavy armor they wore, the knights couldn't swim to safety.

Alecksander's tutelage from then on involved making the lives of others miserable. He hated the things the sorcerer made him do. His veins pulsed. He fidgeted and sweated in the therapist's client chair. His skin both heated and cooled.

Dr. Bower withdrew Alecksander from the past life he visited before he experienced any more misery. "Can you tell me what you saw?" he asked after Alecksander's return to the present.

Alecksander's skin temperature normalized and he relaxed for the first time since before his journey began. He sent an incredulous stare at Dr. Bower. "I was young in another time, and under the teachings of an evil sorcerer."

"Teachings?" Bower inquired.

"He instructed me in the knowledge of the supernatural. At the cost of myself; he forced me to do evil things with my power. I'm not an evil person."

"I know you're not an 'evil person'. Would you care to return to that same time and see how you didn't follow the route he taught?"

Alecksander's body instinctively recoiled. "No. I don't want to see any more of that nightmare." He stood and abruptly ended their meeting. "I think we've done enough for today."

The magician closed the door between him and the therapist with a resolute clunk. *What did Bower say to me to induce such a hallucination?* He didn't know if he'd return. If not for his fixation with Valerie, he wouldn't even consider it.

Alecksander's next regression visit~

"I've done much soul searching after our last session, and I'm back here today to describe to you more of what I saw during my previous regression. I'm also ready to engage in another encounter with my past. Would that work with you?"

The doctor's eyes lit up. He hadn't expected to see his client return after his last regression. Bower recalled how it dealt with memories of whom, he believed, instilled in Alecksander the skills he made his current career of.

After Alecksander spoke of his memories; Doctor Bower tapped his pencil on the desk in front of him and spoke softly to his client, as if in confidence,

"By the story you've just told; I believe we succeeded at our last regression."

Alecksander still found himself in disbelief. "You think I've really lived before? It wasn't a hallucination?"

"Yes. I'm saying I believe you've been reincarnated."

"Whoa." Alecksander sank into his chair as if a two ton weight pressed against his chest. "Is that even possible? He cupped his forehead in his hands. "Never in my wildest dreams did I believe you could make me relive another lifetime.

"I thought your only ability would be to help me remember my past here, during this lifetime. The other had to be a fanciful work of my imagination."

The therapist gave his head a slow nod of acceptance. He went on to give Alecksander a lengthy answer to his question, "In essence; I have to agree with your doubt – to an extent.

"All my past experience with regressing people to their youths, and all my learning in this field would tell me no, a regression such as I told you I think happened with you is not possible, or even feasible.

"I must say what you've just told me is unlike anything I've ever heard of or read about. Even so, we are still early in our regression sessions.

"It could still turn out not to be likely I took you into another lifetime. I think we should continue with the few more visits we have already scheduled, and see where they take us."

Chapter Thirty-Seven

Alecksander cast his therapist a sideways glance.

"Take me, you mean."

Doctor Bower raised his eyebrows and took note of the suspicious expression on Alecksander's face. The therapist tapped a finger on his desk. "You must trust me. I know you have an issue with confidences.

"That's why you're here and we're working together. I thought by now we'd have that behind us." He rose from his chair behind his desk and pointed the same finger into Alecksander's face. "You can trust me. You must accept that."

He leaned toward Alecksander. "I'm here to help you. You're here to be helped by me. I won't sit by and watch while you come to harm.

"A for instance of that would be how quickly I've withdrawn you from your visions when I saw your distress. You must remember I'll always be here to extricate you from the circumstances you see, if they become too unbearable for you."

Alecksander stood and offered a handshake to his therapist. "Thank you," he offered, not certain he could trust this man as far as he asked. His gut reaction spoke to him of betrayal.

In spite of his instinct, though, Alecksander would continue with his scheduled visits. He possessed as much curiosity as his therapist about where his subconscious would take him.

After his final visit, and after his therapist showed himself true to his word, Alecksander believed he could trust again. After all, he'd trusted Bower with his life while he sat helpless in the therapy chair.

He imagined he could trust Valerie that far, too. She'd never done anything that'd warrant his not trusting her; had she?

Alecksander straightened his arms against the steering wheel and pressed back into the seat of his Mercedes when he found his drive home took him to SCSO's office, not to his residence. He stared straight ahead in a trance.

Something has led me to this place. I might as well go in while I'm here. Valerie should be about ready to leave for the day. Would she be willing to speak with him again? He parked and entered the building to find out.

"Hello, Alecksander. We haven't seen you in a long time. What brings you here?" Valerie heard Sandy ask after their front door opened and closed. Her heart rose in a timid state of excitement.

"You've got me. Is Valerie still

here?"

Valerie's pulse quickened. *He wants to see me? I haven't seen him in months.*

"Yes she is. Valerie?" Sandy called out with only a slight raise in her voice.

"Just a sec," Valerie called back. She ran her hands down her sides and over her hair before she walked out of the storeroom she occupied. "Yes?" she wondered in feigned innocence. She skipped a step when she saw Alecksander.

"Oh! I didn't realize you were here," she covered. "It's been awhile. Is there something I can do for you?" Her face warmed at the implications of her question.

"Yes.   There are some things we need to talk about."

"About future engagements, um, entertainment?" She imagined the depth of the rose coloration on her warm face. *I think I should shut up, now.*

A trace of a devilish grin sparked Alecksander's face, and he winked. "Yes." He glanced to where Sandy sat. She quickly looked down to her desk, as if busy with something and not paying any undue attention to their conversation.

He then turned his attention back to Valerie. "We should do this in private; if you don't mind? Maybe over dinner?"

Wonderful. Now what am I going to do?

The smug smile on Sandy's profile betrayed her thoughts about what Valerie should do. "I suppose that can be arranged," she told Alecksander. "I was just getting ready to leave for the day, anyway."

"I guessed that."

Valerie cast him an aside glance, and

left the office with him in tow. They
said no more to each other until in the
parking lot outside the SCSO office.

"It's been a long time. What do we
need to talk about?" she asked while on
their way to their parked cars.

"About the regression sessions I've
attended over the past few months. You do
remember recommending them?"

Valerie's breath caught and she
stopped. *He did go. Of course that's
where he's been.* "Oh! You went. Yes, I
do remember." *As if I've thought of much
else during your absence.*

"I'm glad you decided to go through
with them." *That's an understatement.*
She turned and asked, "Did it work? What
did you find out?"

"I suppose you could say it worked."
Another car entered the small lot and a
couple of women stepped out of it.

Alecksander took a disinterested
glance their way and returned his full
attention to Valerie. "I have a lot to
talk about. It'd be best if we discussed
it over the dinner I mentioned. I know a
quiet place. It shouldn't be too full
right now. It will afford us the privacy
we need."

Valerie deflated. *I can't do that
right now.* "I'd love to discuss this with
you over dinner, but I can't right now."

He raised an eyebrow as if in shock of
her repeated refusal of him. "You can't?"

"No, I can't. There's a little boy
I've taken in to live with me." She
smiled with her mental image of Scotty.
"I've grown especially fond of him. I
need to pick him up at his babysitter's

right now."

"Maybe you can make other arrangements with his sitter," Alecksander stated. He sounded full of unreserved nonchalance.

Indignation stiffened Valerie's spine, but her curiosity about the regression sessions enabled her to tamp it down. *It's nothing personal. He doesn't know Scotty.* "That might work. I left my cell at home. I'll give her a call when I get there. You can follow me."

Valerie considered the evening's new possibilities on her drive back to her condo. After she parked, she left her car and met Alecksander as he pulled into the lot. "If you want privacy while we talk about your adventures, why don't we just have dinner here?"

"I wouldn't want to make your day any longer, Valerie."

"*Really*," She stressed. "It'd be no problem. I can whip up something really quick."

Valerie had her phone in her hand and the number punched-in first thing after they entered her condo. "Hi, Mrs. Feeney. This is Valerie Baldwin. My little boy is in your day care and something unexpected has come up. Could I possibly leave him there at your center a little later than usual?"

"Well, of course you can, dear. We'll have other children here with us later tonight, too. About what time do you think you'll be by for him?"

Let's see, dinner at six. . . "Would eight or nine be too late?"

"No, it won't. That'll be fine. He's such a pleasant little boy. He can

182

join us for dinner. We'll see you later, dear."

Valerie looked over to Alecksander as she clicked off her phone. "We now have a few free hours before I'll need to pick him up. You go into the living room and I'll get dinner started."

"Is there anything I can do to help?" he offered.

"No." She pointed to her living area. "You just go in there, sit and wait for me. I'll be out in several minutes. We'll eat and then you can tell me all about your adventures. I can hardly wait to hear!"

Alone in her organized kitchen, Valerie dashed around and made everything ready. She threw together a salad, grilled some chicken on a portable indoor grill, cooked some fettuccini and prepared a sauce for it.

Now, for some warm bread. She set an Italian loaf she just bought, to warm in her toaster oven. *I wish I had some wine to serve with this.*

"I've prepared a homemade Italian dinner for us," she announced as she carried the dishes to her table.

"Mmm. The aroma is delectable," Alecksander proclaimed as he joined her in her dining room.

Valerie warmed with appreciation. "Thank you." Her expression faded and she issued an apology over her remembered lack of foresight. "I'm sorry, but I don't have any wine to serve with it."

The magician solved her problem with a quick dip of a hand into one of his over-sized pockets.

His action titillated her emotions.

"I must admit; I have missed you," Valerie confided at his easy show of legerdemain.

"And I, you," Alecksander responded in that smooth voice of his. Its sound softened her so her juices flowed in a state of total disarmament. She desired to melt into his arms.

"Alecksander," she returned. All decorum vanished as he enfolded her into his arms and they each held tightly onto the other as if for survival. His lips lowered to and met with hers.

Each of their hands roamed freely over the other's body in a passion that seemed so wrongly denied to them for so long. He pulled away within a moment, his attitude changed, and he broke their shared moment of intimacy, "We need to talk."

"Okay." *He hasn't changed.* "Go sit at the table and I'll serve you."

"Nonsense," he told her as he followed into her kitchen. "I'll help you take it to the table where we'll both be served."

Filled with new hope, Valerie turned at his words, cupped his cheeks into her hands, and gave him a quick appreciative peck on the lips before they continued on into the kitchen.

They washed their hands, and she held up a couple of pot-holders for him to use. "Here, I've prepared Fettuccini Alfredo with Grilled Chicken for our dinner tonight.

"I'll mix the pasta with its sauce and you can take the bread out of the little oven over there, slice it with this knife," she instructed as she put a bread knife into one of his hands and handed him a bread platter for the other. "Put it on this plate."

Alecksander tucked the oven mitts into a pocket and accepted the side-dish paraphernalia she offered. He did as he was told and carried the sliced bread to the table.

Valerie followed him out with the fettuccini, and suggested he grab the salad and its dressing out of the refrigerator while she set the table and poured them some wine.

After dinner Alecksander clapped his hands together and placed them onto the table in front of him. "That was the best dinner I've had in a long time, Valerie."

It surprised her when she didn't see something appear with the action of his swift clap. "Thank you. It's one of my favorites."

"Do you do this for all the men?" he teased after they retired to her den.

"Only my favorites," she joked back. Valerie knew her comment in response held more truth in it than she let on. She noted they still had some time before she retrieved Scotty and so they relaxed into a pair of twin recliners.

Valerie couldn't wait to begin their visit about what, and more, she wanted to know about for a long time. She folded her hands in her lap. "I sensed a change in your attitude when you ended our kiss."

She paused, unsure if she wanted to continue. "It seemed so familiar with the way you were before. Was it? Or did it have anything to do with what you say we need to talk about?"

He folded his hands together on his lap. "No it wasn't and yes, it did.

There's a lot we need to talk about," he reiterated.

His flat words scared her. Her insides quivered, but her hope held on. "Okay. So tell me about everything you said you have to say to me. What have you learned about yourself during our time of separation?"

His hands gripped the arms of the chair he sat on. "I've learned many things."

Valerie couldn't fathom the mystery his voice held. She widened her eyes and took a sharp inhalation. "Tell me."

"First, allow me to caution you."

More fear trickled into her soul. "Why?"

"I learned we are both reincarnated."

Valerie sucked her breath in.

We were together then, and we loved each other very much."

She perched forward in her chair.

Alecksander gave his head a slow shake and held an index finger up in front of her. "Now isn't the time for you to get excited."

Her heart slowed. She let her expression fall, and eased back into her chair. "Why not?"

"There's still more I need to know from you. Now."

Cold dread swept over Valerie at the mysterious still of his cut-off word. "Why?"

She sensed his eyes hardened toward her.

"Our relationship then ended in tragedy with hatred, betrayal, and death."

He closed his eyes along with a quick

shake of his head, as if he shook the vile
things he'd learned away from himself.

Valerie caught herself before she
asked him who did what, to whom. Though
she couldn't make them out, the visions
she imagined within him, chilled her soul.

*His struggles continue. He wrestles
for control. It's best to end this for
now.* "I can see your experience has left
you shattered. Let's end this for now and
speak of it again when you're better
able."

The warmth returned to his eyes when
she released him. "Thank you, but I'm not
sure when I'll be 'better able.' I need
to go there again."

"There?"

"I need to be regressed again."

Valerie's blood pulsed into overdrive
at his statement. "Are you sure that
would be wise?"

A shadowed shade crossed over his
face as if a cloud passed between her and
the sun. "I must if I will ever engage in
a relationship with you. The hatred I
encountered lurks inside me. My trust is
still not solid."

*I've got to get his mind off the
past, at least for now.* Valerie glanced at
her clock and changed their subject, "Our
time is up.

"I need to go get my little boy now.
Would you mind coming along with me? It's
in my building; just a short walk. I think
the change in scenery will do you good.

"I also can't wait for you to meet my
little charge. He's such a neat little
boy." She winked at Alecksander. "He even
fancies himself to be a magician, just like

you."

Alecksander's eyes twinkled. He rose from where he sat and answered her quick word sprint, "There's another magician in your life? I must meet this man. Yes. I'd like to go with you." He followed Valerie out and down the hall.

"Um," Alecksander intoned when Valerie opened the door to the sitter's without it having to be unlocked for her. "No locks?"

The warmth of the secure situation saturated Valerie. "This door opens into the office of one of the larger suites in my building. The children are kept secreted away in other secure rooms." She smiled. "They're quite safe here."

A blond-haired young woman met them at the front counter. "Hi, Valerie.   I'll get Scotty for you."

Alecksander appeared as if he recognized the name.   "Scotty?" he copied after the attendant left them alone. Her eyes widened at his changed demeanor. "Yes. Why do you ask?" she inquired, not entirely sure she wanted to hear his answer.

"The prince's name was Scotty," he uttered.

Valerie tensed with inexplicable knowledge. She remembered the same sensation while he told her of his regression. *He had no mother, just like my little Scotty.* She sucked in her breath. *Is he the same boy and lived with us before, too?*

A commotion sounded as the inner door opened and a blond-headed boy ran out ahead of the attendant. "Hi, Valerie!

What took you...?" He stopped and stared at Alecksander and whispered, "I know you."

Valerie's stomach knotted when she caught the quick exchange of acquaintance between the two. "Um," she stated to Scotty, "He's a friend of mine. You've never met him before, I think. He's the one I told you is a magician, just like you."

At her mention of magic, Scotty turned back into the innocent little boy Valerie knew and loved. She could tell he liked Alecksander because of it, regardless of whether or not he possessed any previous knowledge of the man.

Scotty clasped his hands together in a prayerful mode and pulsed up and down with his knees. "Wow! We can practice together! Huh? Huh? Can we?" he implored of Alecksander.

The magician looked as if he argued back and forth with himself - in the space of a moment - over whether or not he wanted to go there. After his obvious deliberation, he answered, "Yes we can."

Scotty skipped in front of them back to Valerie's condo.

Alecksander chuckled to Valerie. "He appears to be a happy child."

"He is," she answered. Her newest charge's pleasant demeanor, through all the hardships he faced, warmed her. She opened her door to allow Scotty's entrance into her home. Without a word with Alecksander, she stopped and gazed at the seemingly untroubled boy.

Alecksander took her hand while they

stood at each other's side. Her breath held at his action. She looked first to his hand locked into hers, and then to his face. Her hormonal center excited.

He raised her hand to his lips. "It's time I should go now."

"You haven't discussed everything with me, yet."

He blinked. "It can wait."

Then I suppose it is time for you to go," she agreed.

Valerie wished he'd stay and was glad he'd soon be gone, at the same time. She still couldn't be too sure she wanted to hear everything he found in his past. What she did know about upset her stomach.

Alecksander stepped back and swooped in a half-bow.
"Thank you for dinner. It was superb."

"You're welcome. Maybe you could come by tomorrow to perform some magic?" She took a small self-conscious gasp and made a quick addendum, "I meant with Scotty!" *My foot has found a comfortable home in my mouth when I'm around this man.*

Alecksander raised a brow. "Of course."

"'Of course," she reiterated, for lack of a better response.

On the next afternoon ~

Valerie announced to Sandy, "I expect my lunch will be a little bit longer than usual today." She gathered her personal belongings and made ready to leave for lunch.

"Oh?"

"Yes. I've planned a meeting with our entertainer this afternoon."

"And what kind of meeting would that

190

be?"

Valerie frowned back at Sandy's insinuation. "Not what you'd like to think. We just need to iron out a few details."

"About what?"

"About our next engagement with him," Valerie blurted out in a white lie as she made a quick exit though the office door.

She didn't know quite what to expect when she arrived at Alecksander's magic shop. It appeared quiet and unassuming when she entered. She looked about herself in suspicion. The shop's special effects didn't greet her as before.

The office door stood open, but not a sound came to her from within. The hollow sounds of her solitary footsteps, as she took hesitant steps across the room's hardwood floor, were all she heard.

Every sense in her body alerted. Valerie knew anything could happen at any time. Her eyes darted back and forth in the peculiarity of his mystical shop's silence. Paranoia crept over her. She jumped a step back when Alecksander stepped out through the inside of his office as she arrived at it.

She threw a hand up over her mouth. "Oh! Why must you startle me so each time I come here?"

He raised an eyebrow. "It's not something I do on purpose."

"You must've known I'd be here today," she asserted.

"Must I have?"

"Don't answer me with questions." His ways irritated her anew. She poked a finger in his face. "Do not play games with me.

Whether you knew I'd be here, or not, I've come here today because I need some questions answered, not asked."

Alecksander waved an arm back into his office in a gesture of invitation.

Valerie followed his implied request, and stepped past him over the door's threshold.

He followed her in and slid his misted orb from the center of his desk to a spot on its side before he sat behind the heavy furnishing. It imposed on the room with its presence. The majestic desk only cowered under the misted orb.

Valerie debated whether or not to take a seat at the desk, but sat on the straight-backed chair in front of it, anyway. *You want to be cordial, Valerie. You can disarm him in that way.*

Alecksander folded his hands on the desk in front of him as if he'd done this many times before. "Ask away."

She cast all her hesitations aside. "What is this thing between the two of us and why won't you let me closer to you?"

"Thing? You want to be closer to me?"

Chapter Thirty-Eight

Questions! "Your attitude is atrocious." Valerie clapped her palms on the tops of her thighs and stood with the full intention to retain control of this occasion. She placed her palms on his desk and braced herself on them as she stared him down.

"I thought the feeling was mutual." She straightened before him and paced from one side of his office to the other. "I'm sorry I brought the subject up, but I have to admit this thing I mentioned, as much as I don't like it, draws me to you.

"I suspect it does the same to you, whether you admit it or not, but we never connect." She stopped and stared at him. "Maybe we were supposed to connect, but then again, perhaps we aren't meant to be together."

Valerie's anxiety over the whole affair set her feet in motion and she resumed her pace about his office. She soon stopped in another location and again turned on him.

"I suspect, though" she stated, with

her finger again pointed in his direction, "we are meant to be together, and you know what it is that keeps us apart.

"I'm here today to learn the reason we can't be any other than intimate friends. Why won't you allow me, us, to stop withholding our love from each other?" It relieved her she finally had it all out there.

His face revealed no motive. "It's not me," he denied. "I don't know what it is that compels me to keep meeting with you, or you with me. Now would be as good a time as any to have those words with you I mentioned before."

He pointed back and forth between the two of them. "I'd thought my counseling sessions and past life regression would solve all our problems."

She sighed in resignation. When it came to working with her children, Valerie always believed confronting dilemmas when they arose would be the best solution to any problem. Perhaps it'd be best for them, too.

Maybe he's being level with me this time. "I'm sorry your regressions didn't help. We need to put our heads together and think of a solution to our dilemma. Since individual counseling didn't work for you, maybe we should seek couple counseling."

He nodded. "You could be right"

Valerie reached for her cell phone and her list of preferred counselors without any lost time. "I'm not waiting for either of us to have a change of heart. And especially not for you to decide you don't like me again."

"In what direction do you think we should go first?" she asked him while she perused the multitude of names and numbers on her list.

"In what *direction*?" he queried.

"What I mean is, do you think we should initially pursue a relationship counselor or a past life regression counselor?"

"I think we should explore our past lives through regression, first. I've already learned that we've both lived simultaneous lifetimes in the past. Our inner sensitivities already know that by the way we react to each other.

"It's obvious that our present day problems with a relationship must come through the complications of those past lifetimes."

Valerie lightened in an *Aha* moment. "Of course! Once we get the past-life dilemma solved, then our current-day relationship problems should cease to exist of their own accord." She snuggled up to him. "You're brilliant!"

His throaty chuckle aroused her senses to unbearable heights.

****

At Dr. Bower's office ~

"If you will recall, that's what his previous past life regression told him about us," Valerie continued after she reminded Bower, about Alecksander's last visit.

The therapist nodded in recollection. "Given what Alecksander has already learned, we might be able to find your needed answers in one session and solve both your problems with one joint trip into a past life," he told them.

"Let's do it," they answered in chorus.

The Doctor took one of each of their hands and held them securely in each of his. "During this session I want you each to calm down. Relax. Set both feet flat on the floor. Make yourselves comfortable."

With the meditational sounds in the therapist's office of the ancient melodies of a Sitar, Valerie and Alecksander drifted through the air's waves. It lured them both to follow his suggestions with no trouble.

"Close your eyes and drift into a dreamlike state. I will guide you from there. See yourselves on a road, it can be any road. It doesn't need to have any descriptors."

Valerie opened her mouth to speak, but was cut off by the therapist, "No, no, no. Don't comment on or answer my questions, just envision your answers. Where are you?" he paused to give them time for reflection. "Are you alone?" Another pause followed.

"Are you in the past, the present, or the future?" He continued to pause after each of his questions. "As you're walking down this road you see yourselves on, think about where it's taking you."

****

Valerie saw herself as she walked down a dusty dirt road. She couldn't tell where in time she found herself, but sensed the area around her as very far away from her home in Sunview, Oregon. Her

196

surroundings lacked any of her hometown's modern conveniences.

By appearances, it seemed only one other type of life-form occupied the world with her. A camel train silhouetted itself to her in the distance. It traversed over sand dunes on the horizon.

Her skin tingled. She turned in each direction in search of something, anything recognizable, which would set her mind at ease. Though she and Alecksander began this journey together, she couldn't see him now.

Her stamina wilted in the day's heat.

The sands she trod scorched her bare feet. She placed her hands to the sides of her forehead. *Think, Valerie. It could be I'm out in the country somewhere, but it appears I'm in a foreign land.*

Alecksander too, saw himself as he walked down an unkempt road. Ever-shifting sands covered it. In his vision, he saw he walked alone.

By the strange clothes he wore, Alecksander imagined himself to be at some time in the past. He dressed in a medieval-type robe. Embroidered stars enhanced it. The moon and planets decorated it.

His attire felt familiar to him, but different. Though the robe fit him as if tailor made; it suited him as very uncomfortable for the extreme heat he walked in. He remembered he'd always chosen to wear a suit, before.

"Now I want you to tell me about your destination." Doctor Bower continued.

"Where is it? How are you a part of it? What are you doing?"

Whereas her regression became vaguer to Valerie with each step she took, at the interruption of her therapist's voice she remembered her involvement with him. His voice set her heart at the ease she sought. *I'm not alone.*

I approach a hut in what appears to be a small and uncivilized village of several such hovels. I'll be there soon. I can see a castle in the distance.

Chapter Thirty-Nine

Valerie saw no others while she
walked amongst the set of shelters. When
she entered the dwelling of her
destination, she saw the trappings of a
medieval healer - of what sort she couldn't
tell.

Glass vials, chains with charms
attached, and a mirror where she somehow
knew she could see things not visible to
the naked eye, were among the accessories
she identified.

"You in there! Come out!" The
unexpected order came from one who sounded
like some sort of a guard. It jarred her
existence and jerked her to attention.
Valerie sensed her empathic powers were
needed and so proceeded to heed the
demand.

Alecksander saw his destination as

what appeared to be an ancient castle. It
loomed on the sun torched horizon in wait
for him. He knew he lived in the fortress,
and went straight down a flight of great
granite steps when he entered into it.

His steps took him to a cave-like
room where he saw all sorts of magical
paraphernalia. A bell clanged. It broke
the silence of his existence. Someone
wanted to see him and he knew he shouldn't
take long in his answer to the call.

****

Doctor Bower continued his insertion
of questions into Valerie and
Alecksander's unspoken experiences. At
the end of his hour-long session with
them, he brought them out of their self-
induced trances.

"When I count to three and clap my
hands, I want you to sit up straight, look
directly at me, and remember everything
you've experienced about your past life.
One, two, three," *CLAP*! Valerie and
Alecksander both immediately straightened
in their chairs. Each spoke at the same
time.

Bower held his hands up. "Please,
calm down, folks. I don't want you to
report everything to me right now." It
always interested him when his patients
returned to a fully conscious state.

"All my clients react in different
ways as they share their eagerness to
report their vivid memories of trips into
a past life. Your combined reactions
especially pique my interest." He glanced
up and over their heads to his gold framed
oval wall clock.

"Our hour is up. Now I want you to

go straight home and write about your past life without thinking. Put down everything that comes to your mind: actions, words, feelings, dates, etc. Then I want you to read what you've written and meditate on it for meaning."

"Should we do this together?" Valerie asked.

"No. I don't want you to compare notes. What I do want you to do is to bring your writings with you when you return to see me again next week." He clapped his notes taken of their expressions and mannerisms, while they regressed, into a binder.

"We'll discuss and compare your notes on them, then." He stood and extended one of his hands, first to Valerie and then to Alecksander. "I look forward to seeing you both again next week."

They each shook his hand. "We look forward to returning to see you, too, Doctor Dower," they again replied in chorus.

Valerie immediately sat down when she arrived at home and began to write about all she remembered from her regression. Her chest muscles tensed when she recognized a lot of what she remembered from her past life, equated with her current life.

She went by the same name, and she also worked for the government both then and now in basically the same capacity. *And I had loved a magician named Alecksander then, too.*

The similarities between her recently explored past lifetime and this life were just too linked to be ignored. But for all she searched in her mind, she couldn't see what she'd done to make Alecksander react to her the way he did now.

* * * *

Alecksander also processed his regression memory as quickly as possible. His approach to the subject differed from Valerie's, in that he didn't write everything down. He instead gazed into his misted orb of answers and meditated on it for hours.

He, too, evaluated the like connections they experienced in the past lifetime they shared. He cogitated on how they brought those same links forward with them into their lives today.

It didn't surprise him to learn of his past wizardry skills. The knowledge explained a lot of issues, which plagued him all his life. His new information certified he'd been right when he assumed to Valerie he'd always been a magician.

His heart rose in anticipation of the new things he could learn about himself in these sessions. His chest swelled with anticipation. Imaginations of the possibilities multiplied in his mind.

Could there be other lifetimes we've yet to discover? After he scoured his memories, nothing about his current life seemed coincidental to Alecksander anymore. Their further regression sessions would prove invaluable to them both.

The week apart, where they couldn't share notes, passed slowly but surely for each of them. It tormented Valerie. Her heart sped each time she wondered about

Alecksander's regression experience. Her fingers fidgeted to dial his phone number.

She refrained from driving past his home and avoided contact with him for fear of exchanging any information Doctor Bower advised they shouldn't. *He obviously knows more about the subject than I do, and I don't want to mess anything up.*

Alecksander awaited their next regression with unsettled expectancy. His certainty of the visions he experienced wavered. Did he want to attend and learn more about this supposed past life? Did he want to be connected with Valerie?

Chapter Forty

For Valerie; the day of their joint regression session arrived none too soon. She watched the clock all day. Her nervous system wreaked havoc within her as time passed. When the time arrived; she left her condo before the minute went by.

Second thoughts didn't beset her until she sat in her car before she started it. She straightened her arms and pressed against the steering wheel. *What's going to happen? What're we going to learn? Will we find a way to peace between ourselves?*

She held her breath and closed her eyes. *I need to introduce some calm into my soul before I go any further.* She remembered the moments of meditation she'd witnessed in Alecksander, and did her best to mimic his approach.

Within minutes Valerie ended her contemplation and began her drive. She skewed her eyebrows and cocked her head in curiosity when she arrived at the empty parking lot of Bower's office. Uncertainty tensed in her chest.

She scanned the multiplex. *There*

should be other cars here for the other offices in this building. Where are they? Where's Alecksander's?

An uneasy breeze, which matched her emotional state, rifled through her long hair when she at last worked up the nerve to leave her car. Inside the unlocked office, no one sat behind the reception desk. *This is weird. Where's the receptionist?*

She thought of ringing the bell, but stopped her finger as it rose to the task. She looked about the clean office filled with leather-upholstered business furnishings. Alecksander's absence set her nerves on edge. *Will he be here? Is he as anxious to do this as I am?*

Valerie situated herself in a seat on a side wall where she could keep an eye on the desk - and the door. *Has he forgotten? Maybe I should've called him and reminded him.* She kneaded her fingers together and crossed and uncrossed her nylon legging clad legs.

She thumbed through magazines on the corner table. None of the articles interested her enough to read. She rubbed her hands on her arms, inspected the new-age cosmos paintings on the walls, and read through posted patient information.

Nothing would take her mind off Alecksander's suspicious absence - nor the absence of anyone else. In the end she thumbed through the magazine stack again, just so her fingers wouldn't fidget with themselves.

She jumped when the door behind the desk opened. A straight-backed woman with her white hair up in a tight bun, and dressed in a trim-fitted suit, stepped out. Her quiet manner struck Valerie with the otherworldliness one would expect where past-life regression occurred.

"Ms. Valerie Baldwin?" the receptionist asked in a nasal tone.

Valerie sat up straight. "Yes. That's me."

The receptionist sniffed and cast what appeared an annoyed gaze over the empty chairs around Valerie. "And Mr. Alecksander Stone?"

Valerie glanced over to the empty chair beside her and opened her mouth in hopes she could explain his absence.

Alecksander walked in through the office door before any word escaped Valerie's mouth.

"I'm here."

The receptionist raised her eyebrows at his unexpected entrance, and indicated the therapist's inner office door. "You may both go inside now. Doctor Bower waits to see you."

Valerie jumped up to Alecksander's side and whispered to him in an exhilarated release of tension, "I'm so glad to see you here. You're late. I thought maybe you'd forgotten or wouldn't even be here."

He raised an eyebrow to her. "No. I don't forget. I'm always where I should be, when I should be there. I'm not late. You're early," he stated in a flat factual tone.

He held a finger up to her lips when Valerie again opened her mouth. "Calm yourself. I tell you again; I'm exactly where I'm supposed to be, when I'm supposed to be there. You can count on it."

Alecksander stepped back, and with a grand wave of an arm ushered Valerie into Doctor Bower's well-kept office. Floor to ceiling book shelves lined the walls. She noted they seemed filled with books on the supernatural and other like topics.

"Good Afternoon!" Doctor Bower greeted them. He rose as he spoke and indicated two straight-backed chairs kitty-cornered to his desk. "Have a seat. I'm eager to hear about your writings. Did you bring your notes in with you?"

The small stack of note papers Valerie brought with her crackled as she pulled them from her small hand bag and straightened them out to read. She glanced to Alecksander and noticed his lack of notes.

He remained quite still in his chair. *Did he forget his notes? Did he even participate in this exercise?* Her heart arched and she leaned over to him and whispered, "Where're your notes? Didn't you bring them with you? Did you forget them?"

He cast an askance glance at her and twitched an eyebrow. Then he pointed to the side of his head. "They're in here."

"Good! I'm glad you have them." the doctor said. "And what have you learned about yourselves in what you saw? Valerie?" He looked at her with a brightened expression as if he expected to hear much from her.

Valerie clutched her paperwork and perched forward in her chair. "Thank you for choosing me first, Doctor!" She stood and paced about the room while she spoke and waved her arms out to her sides. "I almost exploded with the past week's stress.

"I went right home and wrote about everything I saw during my past life regression. It excited and scared me about the outcome of today's meeting. But let me assure you; I've anxiously waited all week so I could tell you all about it."

Both Bower and Alecksander exhibited a slight smile of what appeared to be enjoyment of her words on the matter. They both nodded to her when she stopped speaking, but said nothing.

The therapist spoke to her first. "Yes. I could tell that you were full of information the minute I saw you come into my office. Why don't you enlighten us with your discoveries?"

Valerie widened her eyes with a mixture of excitement, and alarm - in keeping with her previous words. "What I found felt so right to me, but it was all actually kind of scary. I'm so connected in this life with my past life."

She held her steps in front of Alecksander and looked at him to see if she could read on his face if he'd discovered the same connections. His expression remained blank to her. Renewed fear fueled her system.

Chapter Forty-One

"Connected?" the therapist queried.

Valerie turned her attention back to Bower. "Yes. Well, you see, I was a healer then. I mean, when you regressed me I found myself in twelfth century Rome. I was in a royal Roman court as a healer, and I'm a healer now, too. I work in the Sunview City Court system."

Bower skewed his face in question. "A Doctor, like me?"

Valerie smiled at Dr. Bower and gave her head a slow shake. A strand of her brunette hair dislodged from its brushed back style and fell over to the side of her face. It draped over her shoulder and landed on her chest. "Well, not really like you, but yes in another way. It's a special gift I have."

The doctor's expression never changed. "A 'special gift'?"

"Yes. I possess strong empathy. My ability allows me to see into childhood traumas. I use it in coordination with the Sunview Children's Services Organization.

Valerie widened her eyes and brightened her face as she began explanation about her duties then and now. "To sum it up, it seems I was basically the same sort of healer then, as I am now."

"And did you infer there were other connections you believe might have been there, too?" the doctor asked.

"Yes. I had the same name then. And another connection I found was that I knew an Alecksander then, too." She cast Alecksander a flirtatious smile and gave him a warm wink. "I'd like to think it was the same Alecksander I know today."

He returned a guarded look to her. The shades she remembered he hid under, returned.

"I didn't say it *was* you," she told him. "I said I'd like to *think* it was. The Alecksander I knew then was different." She diverted her attention back to their therapist before she saw any other reaction in the magician.

"Is that all?" Bower prodded.

"Well, I think that was about all as far as the connections go." She paused in thought and then blurted, "Oh Yeah! We both
worked in the same castle and we're working together now, too. That's kind of weird, don't you think?"

"I prefer to think it interesting," the therapist answered. "And what did you find in relevance to your current relationship problems, if anything?"

Valerie shrugged. "Sorry. I didn't find a connection to our current life's problems. I don't remember that I looked for a solution. Actually, I think we desired to be lovers then. As we do now," she mentioned under her breath.

"Something barred us from sharing our passions, though. I can't be sure how close to our current problem the reason for that could be." After the race with her heart all morning, it relieved Valerie to have all she knew out in the open.

Her pulse slowed down and her face heated with 'what if' thoughts of her and Alecksander. *What if we actually did share our previous lives as lovers?* She wanted what she remembered to be true then, as well as today, but assumed Alecksander didn't.

"And you, Alecksander. Is there anything you can be sure about in your regression?" the responsive therapist asked.

Alecksander remained poised and self-controlled as he spoke, "I learned the answers to a lot of questions about myself during my regression. The first being, all my life I've always owned the talent to perform amazing feats of magic, but I've never known where it came from. Now I think I do.

"As Valerie has already told you, we were both 'employed', if you will, in the same castle in medieval Rome. There, I was the highest magician in the court. I was known in that realm as the Master Magician, just as I am known by my public today."

Bower nodded and tapped a finger on his computer keyboard. "And while you were there; did you come up with any answer to your current dilemma with Valerie?" he asked.

Alecksander moved his head in the negative. His expression implied he hadn't looked for an answer at the time, either. "But I too, believe that an unspoken relationship existed between Valerie and me while we were there."

Though his words verified Valerie's initial remembrance of his presence with her in the past, one of his words filled her with annoyance. *Unspoken?*

Doctor Bower rubbed his temple and gave another keyboard tap with his finger. A second later, he positioned both hands over the keys and typed out another note. "So, it appears this isn't going to be as cut and dried as I'd originally supposed."

He looked pointedly at Valerie and Alecksander from across his desk. "Are you willing to engage in more past life regression sessions with me?"

Valerie's muscles surged with her excitement. She gripped the sides of her chair and straightened her arms against it. She nearly jumped out of her seat in the process. "Yes. Oh, yes! I will be here as many times as it takes."

Alecksander didn't move. His monosyllabic response came as, "Yes." Valerie's stomach fell. *He sounds so unconcerned.*

Doctor Bower looked at his watch. "You're in luck. I have time for an extended session today. We can do another regression this afternoon; if that suits you?"

"Perfect!" Valerie blurted. She looked over at Alecksander and hoped her expression implored him to agree. *How can*

*he remain so calm and unruffled about this
whole affair?*

It seemed Alecksander took no notice
of her, or her expression. He closed his
eyes and appeared in meditation on the
matter. When he returned his attention to
them again, he answered, "That can be
arranged."

Her skin burned. The man's patent
answers infuriated her, but at least he'd
agreed.

Chapter Forty-Two

Doctor Bower surged forward as if he seized immediate control of the time available to them. "Let's begin as before. Relax. Breathe. Close your eyes and clear your minds. Don't answer any questions I ask. Just allow them to guide you.

"You're in that same place you were just before your consciousness returned to my office last time. You're in a castle in twelfth century Rome. You wish you were free to engage in such personal pleasurable activities with each other there, as you'd like, but something prevents it. What stops you?"

****

Valerie's heart ached as if torn from her. She stood within the castle walls and watched as her royal magician, dressed in his finest robes, entered the grand room. Her breath held at the realization only mere feet separated them.

She wanted to run into Alecksander's arms and commit herself to loving and giving him pleasure forever, but she didn't seize the moment. Royal rule forbade her from it.

His Majesty's reasoning in his decree confused Valerie. 'Those employed in his royal castle shouldn't become distracted by other interests and neglect their duties to the kingdom.' He'd said as much as he had, and made it into law.

She needed to make him see the error in his decision. But no one could gain an audience to disagree with the king or break his laws, at the possible price of their life. So she and Alecksander were forced to meet and share their love in secret.

Alecksander knew the great importance of his post with the royalty of the kingdom. It required his utmost attention in times of war with other kingdoms, as well as in peace. But he loved the Lady Valerie with a passion greater than life itself.

He showed this station in the royal court as his chosen profession. By the skills of his supernatural abilities; he saved the kingdom from the evil wizard who once held the castle and its people in his malevolent clutches.

Alecksander also accepted he'd need to remain satisfied to share his love with the Lady Valerie in the most secretive places. But she worried him with her impatience. His Lady desired to go against the king and his word.

@She implied she'd face their ruler and tell him of his error. Alecksander knew such an action would only lead to death. His powers were strong, but his weakness lay in his loyalty, which would prevent him from saving either of them.

****

"You may now return to my office in the present time when I count to three and clap. "One. Two. Three," CLAP!

Valerie and Alecksander immediately righted themselves and devoted their full attention to the therapist seated behind his desk.

"Were you able to return to the same previous lives we spoke of earlier?" he asked.

"Yes!" Valerie exuberated.

"Yes," Alecksander replied in his unaffected tone, a moment after Valerie's electrified response.

"And did you find the reason to your problem of being unable to have a relationship in today's world?"

Valerie fisted her hands and pounded the air in front of her. "The king wouldn't let us!"

"It seems," Alecksander began after Valerie's passionate display, "the king wouldn't allow those in his employ to intermingle. Since we were both 'in his employ', so to speak, we weren't allowed to engage in a relationship with each other."

The doctor hunkered over his desk at their words. "Good. We've made progress, but we still need to find the reason for the trust issue between the two of you today."

Valerie cast Alecksander an aside glance. "I still don't know why he has that problem today."

Alecksander placed his confident gaze on Valerie. "I think I do, and I don't think it's entirely my problem."

"Please explain your reasoning to us, Alecksander," Bower suggested.

He looked back to the therapist. "I see it this way. We already know Valerie and I had an emotional attachment for each other in this past . . ."

"Which probably explains why you do now," Bower's eager voice interrupted. Please continue."

"Yes." Alecksander agreed. "With all our other connections to that past, our shared love lives then would seem true." He cast a side glance to Valerie, and returned it to the therapist.

"To continue with my story, it seems I worried about what Valerie considered doing. Her intended action - against my will - promised to bring great pain upon me. That could have led to my current distrust and fear of being hurt."

"And what was it she wanted to do?" the therapist asked.

Valerie's nerves tingled; her memory beckoned. She shifted in her position, cocked her head toward Alecksander, and echoed Bower, "Yes. What was it?"

Alecksander's calm remained.
"Valerie seemed to have it in her head that the king was all wrong in his reasoning for the law, which kept us apart, and she seemed intent to confront him with her opinion.

He shot a stern glance at Valerie. "Disagreeing with the king on his rulings meant death in most cases, if you remember correctly."

A chill seized Valerie. A muscular tremor beset her, and she widened her eyes in disbelief. "Did I get you killed?" she breathed.@

"No; at least not as far as I've

seen." He returned his gaze to Doctor Bower and cast an aside in reference to Valerie, "My trust in Valerie, then, was weak, as it is today."

Valerie's heart fell and she murmured, "What I hear you saying is that our problems now are my fault from something I did in another lifetime."

Samuel cut in, "And that's what we'll explore further on your next visit with me. Shall we say, a week from today, same time?" The two agreed with him and left the office.

Valerie's thoughts whirled on her trip home. *My spontaneity of today followed me from a past life? It made my life unhappy then, just as it has done today? But we weren't always so unhappy.*

Her body overflowed with happiness when she considered how at one time, they experienced trust and love and happiness in their past lifetimes. *But then I went and did something, in my impulsive impatience, which ruined everything then and now?*

What'd I do? Did I differ with the king? Were we both killed on my account? Guilt consumed Valerie over their visit with Doctor Bower. She couldn't concentrate on her work. She lost her appetite. She couldn't sleep.

Chapter Forty-Three

Alecksander's mind busied with many deep considerations of his own when he and Valerie left the therapist's office. Did he really want to know all the past-life secrets he held about himself and Valerie?

An untold heaviness weighted him. The fact he still couldn't grasp what Valerie did to him in his past lifetime, or to them, beleaguered him. A wave of even more uncalled for anger toward and hatred of Valerie washed over him.

Perhaps it'd be best if I called an end to all of this, as I've tried before, and have no further personal meetings with the woman. As first on his new agenda, Alecksander called her organization and canceled all his upcoming fund-raising shows.

He figured that'd ensure he didn't see her again, except for at their joint regression sessions, which he couldn't quit. He needed to know more about the history of his magical skills. *If that means I need to endure Valerie's presence, then I will.*

∗∗∗∗

As since their last meeting, butterflies fluttered around in Valerie's chest on the day of her and Alecksander's third regression session. Her lower stomach hardened with what seemed like a ball of lead. *I need to make things right between us.*

Valerie didn't know why these sensations beset her over a man whose ego sickened her, but for her own sanity she needed to make peace with him. *Our spirits might not ever find the love and trust they seek in this life, if I don't at least try.*

Intuitive knowledge told Valerie he needed her to heal him. *Or maybe I need to heal him for myself.* If she didn't at least put forth the effort; Valerie knew she'd forever be eaten alive by guilt over their unhappiness.

She believed once she reconciled him with the events of his past life, he'd be able to go forward in this life unfettered by whatever she'd done. *Whatever my involvement in this does for me; I at least owe it to him.*

Valerie again arrived first for their next joint regression. She rubbed her damp palms together and down the sides of her slacks. The muscles in her chest tensed. *What if he's decided not to continue with these visits any longer?*

He showed that indication when he cancelled all of his future scheduled performances with the Sunview Children's Services Organization. Now SCSO suffers because of what I did in my past life.

For SCSO, Valerie needed to erase her past transgressions, besides the fact it would also be necessary she find new entertainment. *Will my payment for my actions in the past never end?* Her children suffered for all the shows he cancelled.

They need my healing. He needs my healing. She bowed her head and gripped it between her hands. Her brain ached with the turmoil it held. The burden overwhelmed her. She paced back and forth across the floor of the quiet regression office.

This situation needs to be resolved, and it must be done today. She spread her frantic gaze around herself. Her heart throbbed. *Where is he? Will he be here?*

Her gaze wandered until it stopped and she stared at the clock on the wall. Its two metal hands said two o'clock. *The time of our appointment.* The outer door opened at the same instant. She jumped at the sudden vacuum of its movement.

The knot in her gut loosened itself when she saw who stood there. *Of course, Alecksander is always where he is meant to be, exactly when he is meant to be there.* She caught his eyes. Her insides twisted at their suddenly unfamiliar appearance.

He didn't gaze at her through the sexy and seductive eyes he'd bathed her with in the recent past. Now his eyes appeared to have turned on her in the way she'd feared. "Alecksander?" she asked over the knot in her throat.

"Valerie," he stated, and diverted his attention as if the subject ended.

Doctor Bower entered the room from his office. "I'm sorry about the empty desk; my receptionist is out sick today."

Valerie hadn't even noticed the receptionist's absence while she waited alone in the office for Alecksander. Whereas his literal absence agonized her earlier; now he stood here, the pain of his figurative absence struck her far worse.

Alecksander waited while Valerie followed Sam into his office. Then he followed, as was his custom.

"Have we given any more thought and deliberation to our past lives, as I asked you to do?" the therapist asked in plural to the both of them.

Valerie bolted upright in her chair. Her mind pounded with words to be said, "Of course! There's been nothing else on my mind for the past week, but the need to make things right. How could I have done what Alecksander says?

"The thought that I could have done something bad to the person I love - loved," she paused just a second to pay mind to her words, and continued, "then, has tormented me so much I haven't been able to eat or sleep.

She flailed her arms out to her sides. "I could never hurt, have hurt, Alecksander like he has given mind to." She sank back into her chair in tears. "I'm a healer. I help people, not hurt them," she sobbed.

The heart-throb in Alecksander's throat pounded in his ears. His arms trembled with impulse to reach out and ease

her pain, but they remained held in place
at his sides.

Chapter Forty-Four

Sam stood and reached out to her. "Relax, Valerie," he comforted. "This isn't about you or the person you are, now. I have no doubt you're an exemplary member of our society, and that you were a good person in your past lifetime, too."

Valerie lifted her blurred vision to the therapist. "But what I did then has come back to haunt me," she sobbed. "I lost the love of my life, then and forever, because of that past lifetime.

"Don't you see? I've never been able to find that same love again. And I've caused pain in Alecksander's life! And the children. Can't you see? Everything that's happened is my fault."

Doctor Bower placed one of his hands on her shoulder. Valerie experienced a father's compassion in his action.

She smiled at his effort, dabbed her eyes and nodded her gratefulness for his concern. A sniff overcame her and she attempted to call on her professionalism. "Sorry for my outburst. I'll be fine now," she assured him.

Sam returned to his chair and set his

attention on Alecksander. "And how about
you? Do you have any observations you'd
care to share?"

While Alecksander kept his eyes glued
on Sam, Valerie's imagination ran wild.
*He's ignoring me. After my momentary melt-
down; he probably now thinks the worst of
me.*

Trembles set in again and her
practiced posture softened. *Or worse yet,
does he think I'm right? He probably
wishes he'd never met me. I'm falling
apart over this. Please, God, help me!*

Alecksander's measured words came out
quietly, "I've spent a lot of time in
meditation since our last meeting. I
believe the root source of my inability to
trust and love has come to me from that
past life Valerie and I shared."

Valerie sickened with his words. Her
stomach ached so bad she didn't think
she'd recover. *He agrees it's all my
fault. He hates me.*

"I haven't been able to pinpoint the
direct cause yet, whether it was through
her or not."

A wishful wave of relief washed over
Valerie at Alecksander's words. *They
sounded affectionate and hopeful.*

"But something very bad happened to us
then," he continued. "It forever shattered
our happiness and any chance at love and
trust we might ever have."

"It seems you both still have
unanswered questions. Shall we begin our
next regression session now so that we
might delve deeper into your past lives in
hopes of uncovering those answers?" Bower
asked with his ever eager voice.

"Sure, why not?" Valerie answered, without near as much enthusiasm about their regressions as she experienced before.

"Yes. I'm ready to begin at your discretion," Alecksander told the therapist.

"Then let's begin," Sam advised them. "Relax. Close your eyes. Breathe deeply. Don't answer any questions you hear; just see the answer and follow my guidance." Sitar strains filled the air.

"Where are you now? Are you on that desolate and dusty road out some place where the temperature is unbearable? Do you approach a castle? Are you in the castle? If not; where are you?"

Valerie found herself in the castle in what appeared as a young boy's room. Due to his small size, it took her a minute to realize his existence under the bulky wool blankets draped over him.

She sat by his side and waited for the child to wake, but frowned as she rubbed his forehead. Her emotions ached for the boy and the traumas she sensed he endured. *It's my responsibility to heal him.*

She sought connection with the boy, the evil one she faced in her mind's eye appeared. She knew he caused the boy all his pain. His presence before her set her nerves on the edge of fright.

Valerie straightened and stood. She couldn't sit by and allow the horrible man to do as he did with the prince. She left the boy to rest, and debated on what could be done.

In the trauma of her situation;

226

Valerie struggled over the issues she faced. The prince's fate depended on her - and she couldn't understand the king's reason in barring her and Alecksander from a romantic relationship.

She wanted to stand before the king and present their case to him. Valerie didn't desire to gamble with Alecksander's life, but internal arguments of audience before His Highness never left her mind.

* * * *

As concerned Prince Scotty; Alecksander suffered from agitated nerves at thoughts of what needed to be done, and against whom. He knew there could very well be dire consequences at the confrontation he needed to face, but he'd agreed to assist Valerie in her quest to save the prince.

He respected the Sorcerer, though he despised his ways. He'd once ousted the Wizard Valerie feared, from the castle. His confidence told him he could divert the necromancer's evil ways again, though there might be a price to be paid.

While Alecksander stood in his castle suite in consideration, he also recalled Valerie's spoken solution to their problem. He wondered what her future actions might be.

She is an impetuous sort. Will she go to the king and present our case? Her impulsiveness frustrated him.

Will she venture to tell the king the error of his ruling, regardless of what I've reminded her of? What will be our punishment if she does so? Alecksander wished his magic prevailed over Valerie's sentiments, as it did over others.

When guards arrived, Alecksander knew of Valerie's betrayal. They broke into his suite and fell on him as if on a slave. He used none of his power against them as they drug him out to face the royal ruler.

Alecksander decided; as a good Roman citizen he'd plead his defense before his king and face punishment, if need be. After Alecksander pled the truth, the king dissolved into a tirade.

"You've turned your back on the good of the kingdom. You haven't held the kingdom's best interests at heart! Therefore, by Royal Decree, you are sentenced to die!"

"But Sire!" Alecksander countered. "Are not my unstoppable skills in in supernatural wizardry still necessary to the safety of your kingdom?"

"You can be replaced," the King informed him. To the guards he ordered, "Crucify him for treason!"

Alecksander's opinion of Valerie smoldered with hatred. He knew he should've never trusted a wench with his heart, much less his life. *No one should ever love or trust a woman.*

"Valerie!" he called out in accusation, "I'll hate you into eternity!" In an instant, his inborn instinct for self- survival changed his demeanor. To the king, he directed, "It's a lie! She means nothing to me!

"The wench hath betrayeth me!" Alecksander called out as the emperor's men grabbed him and fought with him to drag him from the king's presence.

While the Roman guards mercilessly wrestled him to the ground outside the castle walls, the evil Mordrid's visage appeared to him. Lightening lit up the skies and The Wizard's wicked laughter crackled through the air.

"Your magic won't save you this time. Neither will it save the child."

Oblivious to Alecksander's vision; the guards laughed as they yanked his arms up over his head and tightened the crucifixion post's bindings around them. The coarse ropes of torture bit into the skin of his wrists and ankles.

Blood flowed from their gashes and trickled down his body to the ground when the brutal guards jerked the wooden implement of torture, with him firmly attached to it, upward.

Alecksander forced himself up with his feet on the pole for a moment of air, and glared at Valerie. She wept on her knees on the blood-soaked ground at his feet. He hoped he portrayed the bitterness and hatred his glorious love for her had become.

He gulped his last free breath a minute before his rigid posture forced his rib cage into a fixed position. It severely inhibited his ability to exhale and denied him another chance for air.

Chapter Forty-Five

An ache as if of a knife's slash through her heart impaled Valerie when she heard Alecksander's tortured breath and witnessed what her unplanned and unconscious actions did to him.

She screamed in horror the moment his body hung lifeless. "Please forgive me! I should've listened to you, but I didn't. You were right." She threw her face into her lap and muffled her final entreaty. "God above; please forgive me."

Valerie searched her mind for conclusion. *How could I have done this to the man I love?* She recalled her lack of focus. *It's as if another will overcame mine. Where was my reason? Was it the shadow within me?*

Her grief invited logic she didn't know existed. *It began the day I meddled in Mordrid's affairs - when I placed my values for justice between him and Scotty. Maybe I should've left it alone; but I couldn't. And now there's nothing I can do.*

Long after everyone else left the scene, Valerie drug her grief-stricken body away into the silence of her dark day. *There isn't any purpose for my life. Why must it continue? I must humble myself before the king.*

"Although you're guilty of the same crime as your lover, you aren't replaceable to me. Therefore I grant that you shall live," the king decreed to her.
"But why, my Lord?" Valerie cried. "I wish to die as Alecksander did."
"The way of your mind is what has saved you. You will spend the rest of your days enslaved in the care of the prince."
Valerie's heart lightened with thoughts of the prince, but only to a slight degree. She couldn't deny the boy, but still couldn't live with herself.
★★★★
The therapist intruded into their regressions when he noticed tears rolled down Valerie's cheeks, "It's now time for you to rejoin me. One. Two. Three." *CLAP!*

Alecksander opened his eyes quickly, but looked away from Valerie and scowled. He shifted in his seat away from her.
Valerie slowly opened her eyes. She cowered away from Alecksander and lowered her countenance, as if afraid to face him.
Dr. Bower reached for Valerie's hands. "What's the reason for your tears," he asked compassionately. "What's happened in your past life?

Great sorrow weighted Valerie's chest on her return to the present. Her lungs

231

ached to add more tears to her already wet cheeks. Only too well; she remembered the time from her past. She couldn't bear to look at Alecksander, nor could she face Bower.

How can I ever accept, or acknowledge to either Sam or Alecksander it was my own darkness seduced me and caused such tragedy? How could I have allowed my will power to be swayed by the shadow I know resides in us all?

I caused Alecksander's torture and death. Valerie jumped and shrank further away from him when Alecksander spoke, without a prompt from the therapist. The magician's trademark calm no longer accompanied him. She cringed at the change in him.

The magician shook with what seemed barely controlled rage. "Now I know, without any doubt, why I've never been able to have a close relationship with a woman," he stated directly to his therapist.

"And why is that?" Bower ventured.

"Because the eternal spirit within me believes women are not to be trusted." Alecksander's cold stare to Valerie stabbed her core. "Now I know why I can't trust *you*, in particular."

Every cell in her body attempted retreat, but she couldn't shrink any further from him. Her chair's confines prevented it. *I wish I'd never been born. Ever.*

Alecksander appeared oblivious to the pain she experienced. He didn't even seem to care about her emotional state as he continued his verbal assault on her. "I loved you once, just as I've tried to today.

"Except now I know I should have never loved and trusted you. You betrayed me. I was tortured and put to death then because of *your*," he emphasized his accusation with a jabbed index finger into her face, "*betrayal!*"

Her throat clogged with her attempt at self-defense. *He knows nothing of my innocence. He'll never be able to accept it and get past what happened to him because of the person I was.*

Too weakened by her knowledge of his hatred, Valerie folded over and collapsed her upper body onto her lap. "I know. I saw it too." She summoned the courage to lift her face and gaze into Alecksander's eyes. "How can you ever forgive me?"

"I'll never forgive you. What will you do to me in this age if I trust and allow you to?"

The chill of his distant voice twisted an imagined blade in her gut. "Please, you must forgive me. This can't go on to control our current lives," Valerie whimpered.

"I cursed you then, just as I curse you now. It's right that you lived, live, your life in loneliness."

"I'll never hurt you again." Valerie murmured in misery.

Dr. Bower once more broke in as a helper through all their turmoil. "Now that we've found the reason for your current problems, you can work on them. Since I'm not a psycho-therapist; you should search one out for trust counseling."

Alecksander stood. "No. I'm finished. Thank you for your time," he stated to Bower as he left the office.

"My life is ended," Valerie cried to the therapist.

"No it's not," he informed her. "Go home and think about this and how it might play into your current life in other ways. And then please, return to see me and we'll work through this together."

"Without Alecksander?" she sobbed.

"Yes. Without Alecksander," Bower stated. "He has his own demons to deal with. I believe I can help you eliminate yours."

Valerie dabbed her eyes with a tissue. She stiffened her spine and took command of her situation in the presence of the doctor's confidence. "That sounds like the solution for me. I can't imagine why I've acted the way I have. Trust me; I'm a much stronger person."

"I know you are."

She glanced at her wrist-watch. "I see I've gone over my allotted time with you. Thank you for these extra few moments. I feel much better now," she told him as she readied herself to leave his office.

"You're welcome," Bower replied as he offered her his hand for a shake.

Valerie dug into her purse when they finished. "Can I offer you something extra for your time?"

"No, consider it my gift to you."

Valerie offered Sam all the gratefulness in her heart with her smile. "Thank you. I'll return after I've done my best to sort all of this out in my head," she assured him as she left for his reception area.

The sun shone down on her when Valerie closed the outer door of Sam's office behind her. She closed her eyes and tilted her face upward to be bathed in its warmth. The bright day lifted her attitude.

She opted to walk back to her apartment rather than take the bus. *Walking will be greener than riding on the bus. It'll also give me time to think without any interruptions.*

Why was I so melodramatic in the therapist's office? That wasn't me. She straightened her posture. *"I'm a free and professional woman who doesn't need a man, like I put on with about Alecksander.*

So what if the woman I was in a past life betrayed him? So what if the man he was then died because of the way that other woman acted? That was then and this is now. It wasn't really me. It wasn't who I am today. His loss.

But he cursed her because of those actions in that past life, and his ill will seemed to have stuck with her. *Enough is enough. The person I am right now needs to spend more time concentrating on the children, and not on Mr. Magic.*

****

Alecksander knew he had his own demons to deal with. *Why'd I turn such unforgiveness onto Valerie? Why'd I leave without a word to her? And why did I choose to make the children suffer by cancelling my fund raising performances for them?*

235

Logic told him what happened in his past life wasn't the fault of the Valerie he knew today. His curse on her then seemed to have stuck, but why did he also experience its end results?

Chapter Forty-Six

Phones rang; keyboards clicked, and monitors surfed. The whirl of activity assaulted Valerie when she opened her office door after her brief hiatus. She'd never seen so many workers busy in the SCSO office at the same time.

The answer to her question came without the need to ask. Scotty had gone missing and no one knew where to find him. *Scotty*. Her Scotty. *Why his sudden increased importance?*

""Why the sudden interest in my little charge?" she asked Carol.

"Someone wants him and we can't find him."

Anxiety fisted in Valerie's chest. "Who wants him?" she asked Carol's back as her co-worker left the room.

"He's done something or needs to be prevented from doing something; I'm not sure which. What's important and that I do know is someone wants to adopt him and for some reason he needs to be found for this person," Carol puzzled on her way out.

My life has become so unpredictable since I met him and that magician.

Whoever wants him must be someone very important for SCSO to react like this. Something has possessed them like never before. I wonder what Scotty's done, or will do?

Valerie turned and left the office to embark on her own search for Scotty. *The time has definitely come for me to experience the problems of children once more, not my own.* Her ability led her to the bus terminal where she first met the boy.

She found the bus in question and climbed up its scuffed steps. "Have you recently seen that little boy we had a time with a while back?" she asked Joe.

"No, ma'am. How've you been, Valerie? Haven't seen you in quite a while."

Valerie nodded and smiled at her dear friend. "It's good to see you again too, Joe. I've been on hiatus."

"What've you been up to?"

She didn't think Joe, in his good old boy way, would be too accepting of past life regression so she simply answered, "Just been spending some time in self-reflection. Getting to know myself better, ya know?" *That wasn't really a lie.*

The driver shook his head and laughed, "Heh, heh, heh. You young folks and your new-fangled ideas. No. I haven't seen that boy around in quite a while."

"Thanks," Valerie mentioned in passing as she turned to disembark his bus.

"Getting off already? You don't want a ride with me today?" he asked.

Valerie paused. "Not today. I'm just looking, but thanks for the information." She left Joe's bus and stopped on the street corner, before she walked home, to gather her thoughts.

She closed her eyes. *You must "see" Valerie. Heighten your senses. You've got to "see" Scotty's traumas. They'll lead you to him.* She froze in place and enhanced her senses to locate the boy.

Her intuitive perception carried her through cold nights and discomfort with the child. When her empathic travels revealed his current dilemma to Valerie, she widened her eyes and threw one of her hands over her mouth. *He's trapped!*

She watched Scotty while he snaked his arms out; as if in an act of sorcery. He pointed to the walls around him and spoke words she couldn't understand. When his attempt at magic didn't work, he kicked the walls. Valerie tensed and fisted her palms.

His inability to escape enraged her. She needed to act and it needed to be done now. *It's a big box he can't get out of. He has to have been kidnapped. That's most certainly why no one's been able to find him. I'm the only one who can find him.*

★★★★

Scotty had no idea why his trick hadn't worked. He circled in observance of the four walls around him. *How'd I get so trapped in this big box?* He'd practiced tricks like this magical mirage many times before, in other boxes.

I've said all the magic words I know. It's always worked before, why not this time? As panic set in, he kicked and hit the box's sides. He screamed for help

until his throat became sore, but no one
came to help him.

*I wish I hadn't found this old box
for my practice of magic. But I needed
privacy!* No one else understood. They
all thought it child's play, but he
possessed power no one else knew about.

He didn't know where his skills came
from, but an ancient wizard in an old
court from so far back in time he couldn't
recognize it, appeared to him in his
dreams. He assumed his skills came to him
from the old sorcerer he dreamt about.

Scotty continued his pounds on the
walls. He screamed his magic words as
loud as he could at them. Finally the
bleak isolation of his circumstances
consumed him. He sank to the floor and
cried.

****

The box Valerie 'saw' Scotty in
didn't appear to be just any ordinary box.
*It's not construction board or plywood or
anything easily defeated like that, which
makes up its construction.* She focused,
but couldn't discern its make-up.

She tensed as memory of Scotty's
fascination with magic returned to her.
She slapped a palm to her forehead.
Of course. How could I have forgotten?

*It could be a magic box, like what
Alecksander uses. That's it! Scotty has
somehow gotten himself into and trapped in
one of the magician's boxes by accident.*

Now she needed to find that box.

It calmed Valerie's nerves and helped
her focus to believe Scotty's entrapment

didn't involve anything more serious. She
hated it, but knew she'd have to contact
Alecksander again.

Her throat tightened. Everything in
every cell in her body didn't want to see
Alecksander again. He'd left her empty
handed with no entertainment for fund
raisers she'd already planned and sold
tickets for.

*But there's no time for that, now.
Scotty's safety must top my list of
priorities. This just happens to be
another time when that man and I need each
other.* She pecked out his number on her
cell phone and placed it to her ear.

"Stone here," he answered.

She choked at the superior attitude
in his voice. *It's been awhile; he might
need to be reminded as to my full and
proper identity.* "Hello, Alecksander.
This is Valerie, um, Ms. Baldwin."

"Valerie?"

Her heart jumped in hopeful eagerness
she couldn't control at the sound of his
voice. *He sounds surprised to hear my
voice. Is it happy surprise?*

"Uh, yes. I have a problem I thought
I might need your assistance with. It
involves little Scotty. Do you remember
him?"

Alecksander's chest knotted. He
remembered once before when she'd asked his
assistance in connection with the small
boy named Scotty. It seemed the results
hadn't been so good that time, but he
couldn't recall anything definitive about
it.

"Yes. I remember Scotty." Sudden

static buzzed in his ear. He wondered whether Valerie could understand his words through it.

"Our connection is breaking up. Could we meet right away to discuss this? It's about the boy's safety." She sounded to Alecksander as though she hoped he wouldn't get the wrong idea about why she wanted to meet with him.

"Yes. That can be arranged."

His words knotted in Valerie's throat. *This must be done.* "Fine. I'll see you at your magic shop in five minutes," she replied and hung up before he had a chance to come back with another casual reply that irritated the pants off her.

Five minutes later Valerie looked up at the clock from where she sat in Alecksander's shop. *The place was unlocked when I got here. But it doesn't seem like anyone's here. Will he really be here to meet with me?*

Why do I always question his reliability? Well, it's really not like he's given me any reason not to question him. I've got to talk to him. If he is even half the worker of magic he puts on that he is, surely he'll be able to help me.

Valerie glanced at the clock again. When she flashed her eyes to the door, it opened. *His punctuality hasn't changed. Did I expect him to be any different?* He still dressed in his dark suit and walked in pompously with trademark cane in hand.

She glanced down at herself and imagined she looked the same as always, too; till dressed as a professional woman in her proper business attire.

****

Alecksander drank Valerie's presence in. *She's still as beautiful as the first time I saw her. But it makes no difference; I've moved on. She'll never hurt me again; I'll see to that. I'll never be hurt by any woman ever again.*

Valerie greeted him before he even got through the door. "Good morning, Alecksander."

"Good morning," he responded as he entered his shop and walked to his office. He entered it without his allowance of her entrance into the room first. After she entered behind him, he took up his position behind his orb and motioned for her to take a seat. "You had a need to see me?" he asked as he lowered his gaze to devices on his desktop.

Exasperated, Valerie burst out for his full attention, "I told you. It's Scotty!"

Alecksander's concentration jerked up to her, as if he'd forgotten. "What about the boy? Where is he?"

Chapter Forty-Seven

"I don't know. He's missing. I left him here with our other homeless children during our regression sessions, but I forgot how inventive he is, and he disappeared."

She tossed her hands to her sides and shrugged. No one knows where he is, but I've had a vision."

"And what is it you need my help with." Alecksander gave a shiver and she wondered at a possible reason. *It must have been his unconscious reaction to me. My assumption about his discomfort with us being together appears to be true.*

She swallowed her apprehensions away and filled him in with what she believed she knew, "My empathic sense has revealed to me what I believe the circumstances of his current trauma are."

Alecksander raised an eyebrow as if in question.

Perhaps he's forgotten my gift. "Of course, you remember I possess a special talent?" she ventured.

"Oh, yes." He responded. She couldn't be sure if his response inferred she were correct in her guess he'd forgotten, until he continued, "You possess the ability to see into children's traumas, and you're able to help them in that respect."

She smiled. It took one more thing off her mind to not need to re-explain her gift to him. "Yes I do, and I've seen Scotty. But I have no idea where he is or how I can help him. That's why I'm here asking you for your assistance."

"Elaborate."

She shrugged her annoyance with him off in silence. "I've *seen* him trapped somewhere. But I can't be sure if he's been kidnapped, or what. I just know he's in trouble."

Alecksander's attention appeared to have been stimulated by her words. "Under what sort of circumstances have you 'seen' him?"

"He's in some sort of a box. I know he's always been interested in simple magic tricks and so I thought that maybe instead of a kidnapping, it could be he's gotten himself trapped inside a magic box somewhere.

"That's where you come in. I imagined you would probably know everything there is to know about magic boxes." Valerie took in the assortment of paraphernalia Alecksander's office contained before she continued, "I was hoping that maybe even Scotty has gotten himself trapped inside one of your boxes."

Alecksander scoffed. It appeared he thought her insinuation ridiculous. "The boy isn't trapped inside one of my boxes. There's no way he could be. No one has access to my boxes, except for me."

She swallowed in fear he wouldn't help her find Scotty. "Excuse me, Alecksander. I didn't mean to insult you or imply you'd allow that to happen. It's just a possibility I needed to explore in my search for him.

"Now, back to the box I've seen him in. It appears to be a very large crate type of container, yet it's different from most. It doesn't appear to be a very ordinary sort.

"It may even be one that'd be impossible to escape from without the use of real magic - like yours. Would you have any idea of, or experience with, that sort of container?"

Alecksander threaded his fingers together under his chin as if he deliberated on the information she'd just given him.

It appears he envisions such a box in his mind. The magician closed his eyes and she watched in silence as he meditated on their problem.

His meditative trait eased Valerie. Her breaths came easier. *He's going to help. It'll be okay.* If he knew of such a box, she knew he'd find it.

Alecksander broke his moment of solitude and pierced his hard gaze through her. "The container you speak of doesn't exist in this lifetime, or this dimension."

A shiver she witnessed across his shoulders piqued Valerie's curiosity. Her heartbeat picked up. She couldn't be entirely certain she liked the alarm in his eyes.

Chapter Forty-Eight

Valerie swallowed down her fear. "What do you mean?" she whispered.

"I believe you know what I mean."

"I do?"

"Mordrid. It could be my curse on you then wasn't the end-all in our eternities. His powers far surpass mine; they always have."

Valerie swallowed hard as she remembered the evil wizard from the regression into her past life. "Why is he involved in this?"

Alecksander sucked in a deep breath. "That's what we need to find out."

****

"I am glad to see you both back," Doctor Bower greeted as they entered his office. "And I'm certainly glad you've changed your minds about further explorations into your past lives, which I assume is the reason you're here?" he eagerly asked as he shook Alecksander's hand.

"Your complicated, inter-connected stories and lifetimes have been on my mind," he offered in what seemed explanation of his gladness in seeing their return. "I hated to see how unhappy you both were after our last session."

Well, we're certainly not much happier now. "Actually," Valerie interjected, "We're not here on a personal basis to explore more about our past lives."

"Oh?" The therapist sounded genuinely surprised, and actually a little bit let-down. "Then what brings you here?"

"A little boy I work, or worked, with."

"A little boy?"

Valerie released a huge sigh of resignation. *This has all gotten so complicated.* "Yes. It's a rather long story."

"Go ahead," Bower encouraged.

"You see, this little boy was actually an unmannered little street urchin when I first met him. But he is quite loveable, in spite of himself," she told her therapist as she remembered her first encounter with Scotty on the city bus.

"I love children and I had myself appointed his legal temporary guardian until I, I mean the organization I work for, could find a more permanent and stable living situation for him."

"You were his legal guardian." the therapist stated in an aside as he typed out a note on his computer.

"Yes," Valerie affirmed. "I took him in to live with me once his homeless situation came to my attention."

"And what is it about this boy that brings you to see me?" the therapist inquired.

"Well, even though this is basically

not to do with us, we've come to see you at this time mostly for the same reason that I've talked Alecksander into coming along for."

"And that would be?" Bower prodded.

Valerie heard the expectation in his voice. "Sorry; I digress. Well, the boy, Scotty, has turned up missing. And if you'll remember correctly, I have a psychic gift where I'm able to see the traumas of the children whom I work with and help them through their life problems."

Doctor Bower nodded as if in remembrance of her gift.

"I've seen where Scotty is, but not really, and that's why we're here together."

"Hmm? You've seen where he is, but 'not really'? Please explain," Bower asked.

Valerie rolled her eyes toward the ceiling in search of the strength she needed to relate her next words to him. "Well, yes. I've seen he's trapped inside some sort of box-like container. At first I thought that maybe he'd been kidnapped and the box I've seen him in was a makeshift prison the kidnappers held him in.

"But then I remembered what his characteristics are, which led me to wonder if maybe he'd trapped himself while doing some sort of trick."

"Some sort of trick?"

"Yes. Well, you see, Scotty has a fondness for magic. He fancies himself as a magician, and he likes to perform tricks."

She gestured to Alecksander, "I

thought the Master Magician here would probably know more about magic boxes than anyone else, so I ventured to him about it."

Alecksander massaged his chin and chose the moment to speak his first words of the meeting. He didn't mention whether or not he caught the sarcasm in Valerie's voice when she mentioned him by title.

"I've meditated on it for a while, and after a moment of deep concentration, I saw where the boy is."

"Which is why I brought him along," Valerie interjected before he uttered any more about his methods.

Doctor Bower creased his brows, which delivered a completely befuddled expression to his clients. "So, if you know where the boy is, why don't you just go and get him? Where does this bring me in?"

"We can't 'just go and get' him. At least not without your assistance," Valerie confided.

"My assistance?" The therapist's confusion appeared to grow at Valerie's words.

"He's trapped in time. Alecksander thinks he might even be in another dimension, with the evil wizard we told you about after our regression," Valerie stressed in an effort to get her point across.

"Oh!" The realization of what they were about to ask him seemed to at last glow for the therapist. It changed his expression. His eyes brightened like a search light. "So, you *do* want to be regressed again.   Not in search of yourselves, but in search of the little boy!" He rubbed his palms together as if in excitement.

"This makes your story even more interesting. I've never been presented with a case such as yours. Three people who've shared the same lifetimes!" It sounded like he imagined the notoriety of this case and what it would do for him in his profession.

Alecksander leaned forward, as if in an attempt to calm the therapist. "Don't get too excited. We don't know he's there for sure. It's just pretty good odds that he's there - now," he clarified.

Valerie hoped his effort to calm Doctor's obvious excitement worked. She watched Doctor Bower frown as he looked at his watch and emitted a heavy sigh. "I'm not quite sure I have time for a regression today," he admitted with a tone of downheartedness.

"Please!" Valerie entreated. She eagerly inched forward on her chair. "Oh, please make time for us. It's very important we find and help this little boy!" For good measure, she added, "Like we lived before; he could be the same little boy who lived with us then, too."

The therapist abruptly straightened in his chair. "Prince Scotty? I never thought of that!" His downhearted expression vanished. He widened his eyes in what seemed appreciation at Valerie's outburst.

Bower lowered his pencil, stood and walked around his desk. He raised an index finger as if he had an idea. "I want you two to wait here for just a few moments.

Maybe I can do that for you, after all. I
need to check this out on my schedule and
see what I can do."

"Oh, thank you!" Valerie's breath
blew out like a balloon in the act of
deflation. Her measured comment worked.

Chapter Forty-Nine

The doctor nodded in acknowledgement of Valerie's thanks and left the room.

"Are you sure you want to return to that time?" Alecksander asked. The wonder in his tone forewarned her of things she might not like.

"Don't forget we're here for the boy's sake - nothing else," she bluntly reminded him.

Valerie stared at his hands in shock when he took hers in his and held them together on her lap. Her heart-rate increased. "I know why we're here," he stated.

"But I'm just beginning to come to terms with what happened to me in that past life. I don't like to hold hatred for you in my heart, but you know another trip back there will open it up again."

Valerie softened her expression toward him. His admittance warmed her all over. "I know what it's probably going to cost us," she admitted. "But you now that the children come first in my life.

"And you also know what my not going

back to help little Scotty is going to cost him." She sighed. "That is who I am. I've got to do everything I can for his benefit. I need to find out why he's back there." She squeezed Alecksander's hands in earnest. "We need to help him."

Alecksander eased back into his chair and said nothing more. She figured he knew there'd be no arguing with her where children were involved.

Dr. Samuel Bower wore a warm smile when he re-entered. His steps bounced. "It's been arranged." The therapist sat in front of them and reached out for their hands. "Let's begin right now," he urged.

"Yes," Valerie and Alecksander again answered in unison.

"Do you remember our procedure from before?"

"Yes," they both answered.

Bower assumed his hypnotic voice, "I'll guide you. Relax in your chairs. Don't attempt to answer any of my questions; just allow me to guide you along. Close your eyes."

Melodic music soon filled the air. "Listen to my music as it plays. Allow it to carry you back in time to your original destination. Once you've reached the castle, remember who you're looking for."

★★★★

Scotty! Valerie could think of nothing else. She ran up the lengthy stone staircase to his rooms. A breeze blew through the purple drapes on the window. His bed appeared unslept in.

Inconsolable emptiness tore at her heart. Fear rushed up through her chest in a channel of nerves. Tears blurred her vision. Her anxiety clenched her hands into fists.

Where can he be? She sent frantic glances to all corners of the chiseled stone room she stood in. *I must find him.*

A vague image of something or someone yet to be flashed through her mind.

Its brief appearance vanished as fast as it appeared. She shook it out of her head. The time didn't exist for her to spend on the eerie discomfort it beset her with. She needed to find the prince.

Valerie left the royal bed-chamber behind in a frantic chase. The loose-draped cotton stola she wore billowed as she dashed out the door. She stopped in frustration and sat on the highest step at the top of the marble staircase. She held her head in her hands. *I don't know where to go. I've got to see.*

Concentrate. See. Scotty's fright appeared in her mind's eye within moments. Her heart ached at the vision. What she beheld of his trauma also showed her more of the room he occupied.

It didn't appear to be a large room, but the box he existed in did seem to be impenetrable. *But where is this box?* She courted a second thought at her wonder. "If it's not Alecksander's, whose box could it be?" How did she know it wasn't his?

Oh, *Dear God; I need my Master Magician.* A knot formed in the pit of her stomach at the impossibility of her desire. *I need Alecksander's help, but he's already been put to death. A death caused by my uncontrollable urges.*

A rush of air billowed past her as if the large double doors of the castle burst

open. Valerie's heart leapt and her
emotions rose out of despair. *Someone has
come!* She stared downward toward the
doors from the top of the massive stone
staircase.

Valerie's heart chilled on her intake
of air. No one stood there; the castle
doors remained locked. She strained to
see who might have caused the disruption,
but didn't see anyone near the doors. Her
heart returned to the basement of her
psyche.

Chapter Fifty

His head hazed. Vapor misted his
vision. *How'd I get here? Where'd I come
from?* Shadowed essences he felt one with
surrounded him.

He looked down in question at his own
body. It appeared as vaporous as those in
the mists around him. Realization stilled
him. *I'm a ghost. They killed me.
Valerie killed me.*

Alecksander's remembrance of her
complexity in his death burned through his
soul. A small quiet knowledge inside
informed him he returned to help her.
*Help her? Why would I want to do that? I
cursed her to live a lonely eternity.*

He heaved the great tonnage of the
castle doors open to their fullest extent,
with no more effort than if he pulled a
silk drapery aside. A great vacuum of
souls swooshed past him through the chasm
created by the castle's opened doors.

Alecksander beheld Valerie's lovely
form before he recognized anything else.
Lovely? The one who betrayed him and their
love. *Love?*

Hatred hardened Alecksander's soul.

257

He'd never love her again, and neither
would she love anyone else. His unearthly
status told him his curse from before held
true. He foresaw its permanent attachment
to her through all her incarnations.

He knew he could remain firm in his
detest of her on the other side, and
sought his return to it. But a struggle
ensued when he girded himself to meld with
the state of nonexistence he came from.

A power far greater than his own
propelled him toward her. It filled him
with the knowledge he would help her. He
closed his eyes, as he'd done many times in
the past, and pondered on her need for his
assistance.

The vision of a small boy from a
future lifetime developed in his mind's
eye. The sight quickly dissipated and a
vision of the young prince replaced it.

*His soul lightened. It's the boy who
needs my help. Scotty's the reason I'm
called back from the grave, not Valerie.
My opinion of her need not change. I will
hate her forever.*

But he would help her. Alecksander's
decision enabled his remembrance of the
evil Valerie spoke to him of in previous
times. He filtered inside, to the castle
foyer.

A deep sensation of sadness warped
through his being with his entrance. His
whole essence twisted with Valerie's pain.
*Why should I care if she cries? She should
suffer as I did, but the prince needn't
suffer.*

Where is Prince Scotty? Valerie's
tears told him she didn't know. Instincts
told him Mordrid's whereabouts would be a

good place to start.

He called out to Valerie from where he stood. She raised her attention, but only sent a blank stare in his direction. Alecksander could tell she recognized his presence. *She knows I'm here; why won't she speak to me?*

Of course; I occupy a different plane of existence than she does. The vibration of my call affected her. She doesn't know it's me. He moved to her side, but she passed through him when he tried to touch her.

Somehow I've got to direct her. In the only way he knew how to do so, Alecksander cloaked his otherworldly existence around her and guided her in search of the boy.

Valerie's senses wavered and drifted. Her vision blurred then defined. A will beyond her solid state of reason beckoned. The motivation came over her much the same as caused her earlier petition of the king.

Without question, Valerie stood and allowed herself to be guided forward in descent of the massive staircase. She traveled as if in a sleepwalk.

She paused when she stood at the now opened grand doorways and looked out onto the kingdom spread out beyond the castle walls. In her obeisance of whatever propelled her, she wandered through the castle yard and into the village.

A quiver beset her when she saw she approached the domicile of the fallen evil wizard. She faltered in her footsteps and fought to turn back, but held no will over the way her feet took her.

Her impulses prevented her entrance into the forbidden lair after she reached it. She instead walked around the dismal domicile and found a large block of marble behind it. The compulsion to move further vacated her in its presence.

I'm no longer being led. She stepped carefully around the questionable rock. *It appears as if it could be a natural formation.* A vague remembrance fleeted through her mind. It hovered on the edge of her consciousness.

Who brought me here, and why? She sent her vision from side-to-side and top-to-bottom over the boxlike block in front of her. *Is there something inside?* She focused her senses and peered within its interior.

Her heart squeezed without mercy at the vision her concentration brought to her from within the confines of the huge stone mass. *The little prince is trapped inside!*

Every ounce of desire within Valerie wanted to hold the little boy and love him. He needed to be comforted by her. *I need to save him. I must take all his hurt away.*

A whizzing whoosh of horror took her next breath away. She could no more than watch as the Wizard's ghastly form appeared inside the box with the small boy and traumatized him.

****

Alecksander knew exactly where they should look when they arrived at the place where the Wizard resided. After he recognized the entombment the evil one kept the boy in, he knew the time arrived for face-to-face confrontation with his mentor.

The Master Magician left Valerie to her own devices outside the block of marble, and appeared inside the block the same way as Mordrid did. His blood boiled when he saw the prince huddled into a corner with the evil wizard, who hovered over him.

At that moment, the prince looked up and Alecksander recognized the little street urchin from the future. He sat confined in his own small cell there, too. Now Alecksander remembered everything.

The therapist from the future was right. Valerie and Scotty and I are all connected through time and space. Alecksander knew he needed to save this little boy so they could return to their existences in the future.

He summoned all his power. In a starlight flash Alecksander appeared before Mordrid.

Chapter Fifty-One

CRACK!

Valerie pulled her awareness from inside the rock and back to its exterior as her vision shattered. The large stone leaned and towered over her. It shook and fissures appeared in its mass.

She cowered back. *Control yourself, Valerie. Scotty's in there. You must save the Prince. But I'm alone. How will I do it?* Her heart fell; she'd convicted her only source of assistance.

The massive marble creaked and groaned. The ground under Valerie's feet vibrated and cracked. She envisioned showers of rock would soon fall onto her.

Valerie centered her vision and drew on everything inside her to see. No visions came to her. She increased the intensity of her stare into the rock in front of her - still nothing.

She raised her hands to the Heavens. *What can I do now? What's happening to the little prince now? What'll happen to him if this boulder bursts?*

****

Mordrid's ominous form loomed. He shadowed both Alecksander and the boy. His malevolent voice bellowed toward Alecksander. "Who are you to think you'll be able to stop me with your insufficient abilities?"

The walls quaked around them with each word the sorcerer breathed. Fantastic fragments of supernatural supremacy rained down on the two smaller beings with him.

Alecksander grew in his own right, though his size didn't match Mordrid's in dominance. "I will stop you!" he thundered.

"A-HA-HA-HA!" The walls around them shuddered at Mordrid's malevolent laughter. "You weren't able to help yourself or your lover when I possessed her and she caused your death by her own words! And now you're both cursed by *your* words! A-HA-HA-HA!"

Alecksander's anger fired over the eternal fate Mordrid dealt him and Valerie. And now the ancient wizard sought to deal out another horrible destiny to the little prince and his future presence.

Alecksander's cane glowed with a fierce majesty of its own. Fire and sparks shot from it toward the evil Wizard. The Master Magician's integrity combatted the glaring stream of wickedness, which oozed from Mordrid's green eyes.

****

Valerie ran to the marble slab when the massive rock's movement stopped. *What's happened?* It terrified her she couldn't see what took place inside. She pounded on its sides in hopes it would release her little Scotty. "Release him!"

The block responded with a mighty
surge of energy. Its unexpected
immediate quake hurled Valerie backward to
the ground. She rolled her face into the
grasses where she laid. Her muffled
screams were all she heard.

Her screams soon turned to sobs. *That
poor little boy, I can do nothing for him.
I wish Alecksander were here.*

The ground beneath her trembled. The
marble's uproar grew until it exploded. In
the midst of the fragmented shards,
Valerie scrambled to her feet and ran to
find Scotty.

Her heart shattered and she fell to
her knees amidst the burst stone when she
didn't find him. *Did he explode with the
stone?* Horror at the thought kept her from
breathing.

"We're here."

Chapter Fifty-Two

Valerie's heart skipped. She couldn't believe her ears. *Alecksander?* She twisted around to see the voice's source, and dropped from her knees to sit.

Do my eyes deceive me? Not only Alecksander stood behind her, but Scotty, the little boy from her future stood by his side. "You're alive," she whispered; still unable to believe the blurred vision she saw through her tear-misted eyes.

An emptiness she'd never before witnessed in Alecksander's eyes sent an immediate chill through her. *He's not the same.*

"In a way, yes I am." he answered, as if he held a secret.

Valerie gazed at him from beneath her eyebrows. *What did that mean?* "What do you mean?"

He didn't have a chance to answer, even though Valerie wondered if he planned to, before Scotty sprang into action. He ran to her side and threw a big hug around her legs, hidden under the drapes of the cotton wrap she wore.

"Valerie!"

She burst into immediate tears of joy and bent down to encircle him with her arms. "I'm so sorry I allowed this to happen to you," she apologized.

"But now I can do *real* magic!" the little boy squealed without obvious notice of the changed time he stood in. "That old evil wizard messed with me so much that some of his powers rubbed off on me!

"Look!" he directed. Scotty pointed into the debris and an impossible fire arose from the scrambled stonework.

"Ah! You *do* have magic!" Valerie wholeheartedly agreed.

"It was his magic that saved our day," Alecksander said.

"Yeah! I combined my magic powers with the Master Magician's and we defeated that old Mordrid!" Scotty explained. "That mean man won't hurt children anymore."

Mordrid's death set them all free of the curse. Valerie's eyes opened her to a wonderful new life of opportunity, not one of personal loneliness. The heaviness she endured through all her trials existed no more.

Valerie held Scotty close to her. "No. He won't hurt children any longer." She grasped the boy's tiny shoulders and held him at arm's length from her. "And he won't hurt you anymore, either."

She looked to Alecksander. He still stood where she first saw him, but his form became vaporous as she watched. *It's like he appears to me from another world - like a ghost.*

The thought sent shivers through her,

but she sank into denial and refused to acknowledge it. Her lips quivered. "And he won't hurt us any longer, either," she told him.

"Mordrid will never hurt anyone again," Alecksander responded. His voice sounded as if it came from deep within a vacuum. "I've been convinced of what he did to us. It's been Mordrid's curse all along.

"It's a thing that I've considered before now, but something in me wouldn't allow my full belief in it. I'm sorry I've been so blinded by my selfish hatred."

Valerie's lips trembled along with her heart. She didn't know whether she should feel joy at what Alecksander said to her - or not.

"While I was in there with him, he admitted to me what he did that led to my death. Now I know for sure. It wasn't your fault. I've banished that shadow; my hatred for you is now gone."

"Yes!" Valerie stepped toward him, but he backed away. "Come over here to us," she entreated of him.

"I can't."

She stood, but didn't release Scotty's hand. "Then we'll go to you."

"You can't."

"But why?" she asked as she and her young charge both took a step toward him.

"I'm crucified, remember? Mordrid's death at this time doesn't change that. But neither of us will suffer any longer."

"How can I not suffer when you are dead by these lips," she asked as she touched her mouth. "These lips that've

267

only lived to kiss yours." Her memory unlocked and she knew of all their lifetimes.

Her adrenalin surged. Her muscles endeavored to leap from her body. "We must take this boy and return to Doctor Bower's office! We aren't dead there and Scotty needs our love and care in the future."

"Yes, we must. Scotty has been freed for his next incarnation, and we can't return without him."

"Huh?" Scotty asked Alecksander. "My next 'carnation'? What's that?"

"You are now a magician, just like Alecksander," Valerie covered. She knew Scotty was too young to understand everything. She retrained her vision on her Master Magician. "Now we need to find a way to get Sam to bring us out of our regression."

****

Doctor Bower took a great interest as he watched Valerie and Alecksander in their current session. Their actions at this late time in the regression especially intrigued him. The roles they now played switched from previous times.

Alecksander became the more aggressive character, and Valerie assumed the more passive role. At times Alecksander appeared as if he performed or executed great feats of magic, while Valerie appeared clueless.

Suddenly they stopped their actions and stared their seeing, yet unseeing eyes straight at him. Valerie's body tensed and almost leapt out of her chair toward him.

It has to be a sign. The time has

come for this regression to be ended. "A clap at the count of three," he told them.

"One. Two. Three." *CLAP!* Their eyes focused and it appeared they saw him, instead of whatever it was they last looked at.

Valerie completed her jump from her chair and immediately blurted out, "Scotty has been freed! We have to find him!"

Chapter Fifty-Three

Sam tilted his head toward Alecksander.

"My hatred of Valerie has been banished," Alecksander told him in a much more reserved manner than she. "You were right. We've both lived before in connection with Scotty. Now we must find him to make the circle complete."

Doctor Bower's eyes lit up. "And where is it that you believe Scotty should be looked for?"

Alecksander rubbed his chin. "We know where we found him during our past lifetime. In order to find him now, I will need to spend some time in meditation with my misted orb,"

"No," Valerie intoned. "I mean yes! You spend some time in meditation and search for his whereabouts. By no, I meant that there is no way he could be in the same place or with the same man as he was then. Could he?" She received no answer.

Alecksander instead stood and offered his hand to Sam for a shake. "Thank you for all your time and guidance in this maatter."

Valerie followed his example and offered her hand as well. "Yes.   Thank you Doctor Bower."

"Are you sure that'll be all?" Bower queried. "I'm quite taken by your interesting story and would love to know more. Would you be interested in learning about other lifetimes you might have lived together?"

"We've found the answers to our problems from that one past life, and I'm sure we can handle our current lives from here on without adding more at the moment," Alecksander assured him.

As they readied to go, the therapist told them, "I wish you two all the luck and success in the world. You'll be back if I can help when you find him?" He threw in as they left his office, "Please contact me if you change your minds about more regressions or need anything else that I can assist you with."

As they left the therapist's office, each knew a new man and woman walked away. They had so much life to live, and so much love to give.

Alecksander stopped outside the building and drew Valerie to him. "It's been a long time," he whispered as he lowered his lips to hers. The passion in their kiss equaled no other they'd ever shared.

Valerie broke their kiss with the impatience of a momma bear. "Scotty comes first!" "Right now you need to drop me off at my place so that you can go to your office and meditate on his whereabouts with your orb of answers. We must find him, and soon!"

"I suppose you're right," Alecksander agreed in a monotone. It seemed to Valerie, other things occupied his mind at the moment.

They continued their trip to his car and he opened the passenger door to let her in before he went to his side and got in. Valerie loved the soft leather seats in his Mercedes. She snuggled in and appreciated the warmth in them generated by the car after he turned it on. The coldness of the Northwest November day they returned to vanished.

Alecksander placed one of his hands on her left thigh and leaned over for another kiss.

Valerie giggled and wagged a finger in his face, "Don't get started. We've got business to attend to."

"Of course," he agreed as he shifted his car into gear and pulled it out onto the busy city street. The drive didn't take long and they soon found themselves parked in her condo building parking lot.

"Are you coming in?" Valerie asked when he shut off the engine.

"No, but I thought I'd escort you to your door."

She reached for her door's handle.

"Remain seated; I can get that," he stated as he left the car and walked around to open her door, as he did many times in the past.

I could become so spoiled by his gentlemanly gestures. The November chill smacked Valerie in the face the instant she left the car. "Why don't you come on into my place with me for a minute? We can warm up and I'll fix us something hot to drink before you leave."

He followed her into her kitchen and watched as she set the thermostat to warm her cold home up. Then she started some coffee to brew. "There. That should be ready in . . ." She turned and Alecksander's lips met hers.

Valerie savored the surprise. His kisses were now so much different than before. While they'd always been passionate, she couldn't remember all the love and tenderness they now possessed.

"I'm sorry I keep ambushing you, but I can't help it. Now that I have the capacity to truly love, I only want to bestow it on you with all my time and care," he murmured against her neck.

She relaxed into more of his kisses and shared her newfound ability to love, with him, too.

"The coffee can wait," he told her as he ushered her into the next room.

"Oh, yes," she breathlessly agreed.

He already had her jacket unbuttoned as he guided her down to sit on her sofa beside him.

She busily unbuttoned his shirt and pushed it off his strong shoulders as he caressed her breasts. Neither needed to urge the other as they laid back on her soft piece of furniture in unison.

Soon they abandoned the remainder of their clothing and relished the sensation of their skin on skin as they fondled and caressed each other with their love and affection.

He blew softly into her ear and whispered to her, "I have waited so long for this."

"Me too," was all she could manage as her new found ability to engage in lovemaking, with the man she'd waited for all her life, consumed her.

"I must have you, now," he groaned.

"I'm all yours," she permitted.

How long their love-making continued was of no consequence to either, and neither knew the length of time they remained in the throes of their long awaited passion.

★★★★

Valerie awoke to the smells of coffee and breakfast. Bacon sizzled and the aroma of baking biscuits wafted out to her.

Chapter Fifty-Four

Alecksander walked out of the kitchen and into her bedroom while he wiped his hands with a kitchen towel. He appeared resplendent in Valerie's red checkered apron.

Her magician kneeled by her side of the bed. "Good morning, Sleeping Beauty," he murmured as he nuzzled her cheek.

She jerked to attention and looked out her window. "Morning?"

"It seems that we were both much more exhausted than we imagined. We slept through the remainder of yesterday and all through the night after our long awaited enjoyment with loving each other."

Valerie loved the way he liked to talk to her. "Smells good," she complimented as she rose and held a blanket to herself. "I'll just be a sec," she said as she scampered off to the bathroom.

After breakfast Valerie kissed Alecksander good bye at the door as he left for his office. She giggled and hugged herself. Her once lonely life would never be the same again.

She slipped out of the happiness of her newfound reverie and reminded herself she'd soon need to get to her own office. *Scotty needs to be concentrated on now. I've been selfish for too long.*

She needed to find out if anything about Scotty's case turned up during her absence. It might assist them in their search for him.

* * * *

Alecksander couldn't remember ever having been happier as he drove to his shop. *I've conquered my past.* Now he could concentrate on a new future, one that involved the woman he'd always been meant to love.

But first we need to find Scotty. We found him and freed him in the past, now he needs to be found and released in the present. Alecksander hoped what occurred in the past already set the boy free.

At his office Alecksander gazed into his misted orb and prepared himself to find the answers it held for him. Its multi-colored vapors gathered and swirled, cleared, and came together again.

Nothing came easily visible to him. His meditative thoughts gathered and swirled and misted the same as those in his orb did. *Its message has never before eluded me as much as it does now with my questions about Scotty.*

A glimpse of what it endeavored to tell him flashed before his eyes, but then vanished into obscurity as soon as he devoted his attention to it.

The orb darkened and then blanked to white. A vision of black and white came to him time and time again. Soon it too, vanished. *What's it trying to tell me? What's preventing it?*

✶✶✶✶

Valerie found nothing about Scotty turned up during her absence. When she left for the evening she had high hopes Alecksander's meditation with his orb divulged the solutions they needed for their problem.

A lighted intersection stopped Valerie and her eyes locked onto the pedestrian who crossed in front of her. He looked all very proper, dressed in a white lab coat. What caught her attention about him were his tall black boots.

His footwear extended up under his long white coat. He also wore a large black hat with a wide brim. *He looks like he's wearing camouflage. What's he hiding from?*

Though she didn't consciously recognize him; the man's familiarity struck her. *I've seen him before. I should be aware of his identity.* Images of the man in the white coat nagged at her until Alecksander arrived at her door that night.

"Did you find the answers we need?" she asked before he even had time to enter her condo.

He appeared confused. Instead of an answer to her question, he spoke of his day, "Time spent in meditation with my orb has always provided me with the answers to problems I've presented to it in the past." He shrugged. "But not this time.

"I spent most of my day in deep

meditation with it, and all it presented was a vision of black and white." He shook his head. "I can't, for all the reason I possess, conceive of what it could be trying to tell me with that vision."

Valerie's heart lurched. She gripped a piece of the iron ornamentation on her entry-way wall. *Black and White.* "Those are the colors that've been stamped on my brain since my drive home," she breathed.

By his pointed stare, Alecksander's attention seemed to be piqued with her words.

Valerie immediately answered his curious expression, "On my drive home, I was stopped at a light when a very curious looking stranger crossed in front of my car."

"Curious? In what way?" he asked.

"He appeared to be some sort of a scientific guy and seemed to be dressed very proper in his laboratory coat. The rest of his attire, and the clandestine air he possessed, is what struck my intuition as abnormal."

"How's that?"

"In addition to his coat, he wore tall black boots and a black hat. It seemed he hid under it. I haven't been able to get that man off my mind since I saw him. My stomach niggled at the time and told me that I either knew him, or needed to find out his identity."

Alecksander took his concentration away from her and gazed out her window as if he mulled her words around in his mind. "We were both impressed with visions of white and black today," he mumbled.

"What do you think it means, if

anything?" Valerie asked.

.

Chapter Fifty-Five

"I'm not sure. It does mean something, and that something is what we need to find out. I'll engage in more meditation and ask my orb about it. I know it desires to alert me to something," he said as he turned for the door. "I'll attend to that now."

****

After an uninformative evening, and a sleepless night, the next morning found Alecksander back at his office for another day's long session of intense meditation. His misted orb of answers didn't seem to be hampered on this day by what prevented it from communication with him on the previous day.

At first it misted and gathered and swirled bouts of mystical vapors, but soon settled down. The screen darkened to black and then blanked to white. A vision in white and black appeared to Alecksander from within his orb.

The Master Magician strained and used all the power in his supernatural mentality to latch onto the appearance before it dissipated into the mists. *I was correct in my assumption; it was a man I glimpsed within my orb. And the man matches Valerie's description of who she saw and told me about.*

Alecksander refined his focus, peered deeper, and scrutinized the persona his orb held for him to see. The man did appear to be dressed as some sort of scientific professor, and he appeared as if enroute to his lab.

A very tall, out of place, blockish building loomed in the distance. Alecksander's chest shivered in remembrance of the large rock from the past.

He widened his eyes just a bit as he watched the man. Instead of going to and entering the building in the usual method, the black and white dressed stranger lifted an inconsequential manhole cover in a side alley.

Alecksander watched as his suspect paused with the cover in hand and looked about himself. It appeared he watched to see if anyone saw him. Apparently satisfied; the man then descended into the building's underground. The cover lowered behind him, as if by itself and without a sound.

Alecksander saw the man's face before he vanished underground, feet first down an interior ladder of sorts. He recognized the enigmatic stranger by his piercing green eyes. They glowed onto their surroundings. *It's the wizard.*

Adrenalin thrilled through Alecksander's chest. *But we destroyed him. He's dead.* The magician sprang to his

feet. The orb and its table jostled back
to a balanced position when he pushed them
aside and ran out the door to find Valerie.

"Will these connections never end?"
he asked Valerie as she opened her door to
him.
"What're you talking about?" she
hesitantly asked. "What'd you see in your
orb?"
"I think I've discovered who our man
in the white lab coat is. I caught a vision
of him in my orb; that's what I'm talking
about.
"It seems that the wizard from our
distant past is also connected to us
today," he continued into her pale face.
"But I thought you and Scotty
destroyed him."
"We thought so, too." He shrugged.
"But if our spirits can travel around in
time, so can his, I guess."
Valerie took a shrill inhalation. "Is
he the one who has Scotty?"
Alecksander's gaze pierced into her
eyes. "Yes. I believe I've found the
boy."
Valerie leapt toward Alecksander and
placed her fists on his chest. "Where is
he? Where's that man got Scotty?" she
insisted.
"He's kept in a place against his
will with a host of other children."
Valerie widened her eyes. "It seems
that evil man has always existed to hurt
children.   What kind of place is it he
has them? Where's Scotty?"
Alecksander paused. He looked
everywhere in the room, except into her

eyes. By his mannerisms it appeared he needed to tell her more, but at the same time it seemed he didn't want her to know.

"It's not a good place."

"Where is it?" Valerie pleaded.

His eyes finally lit on hers. "I can show you."

She bolted toward the door. "Well, come on, then! Let's go!"

****

They took his car and drove through the eerily quiet city streets. Alecksander didn't consciously know where he was about to take her, but he followed his subconscious. It knew.

He frowned and Valerie shivered at the direction they drove. He sensed how her hopes lowered as the filth of their surroundings intensified. Soon, as if of its own will, his car stopped.

An extremely large and very old building existed outside their car. Shards of metal panels hung precariously from its sides. Cracked windows stared out at them.

Alecksander opened his door and stepped out of the car. "Wait here."

Valerie threw her door open, shoved herself outside and slammed it shut behind her. The sound echoed between the buildings on the empty city street. "I will *not* 'wait here'!"

Alecksander turned and willed her to stay put. "Valerie. You don't understand the power of the realm I'm about to enter. It's too dangerous for you."

It seemed her next words were sent to remind him he possessed no authority over her. "And you don't understand the 'power' of the emotion I'm driven by to

283

rescue Scotty."

He glanced upward in frustration. "You can't go in there with me," he stressed. *I must reason with her.* Valerie had her hands on her hips by the time he lowered his gaze to her.

He reached out and put his hands on her arms. "Don't you see? I *do not* want you to go in there with me. I might not come back out alive. Scotty might already be dead," he stressed. "What good will it do any of us if we all three are dead?"

"But Scotty might still be alive!"

"And if he is, I'll return him to you."

"But if you're dead."

"Stop it! You need to wait and be here for Scotty when he returns to you."

****

Valerie silenced. She saw an inferno she'd never witnessed before in Alecksander's eyes. That and the urgency in his tone gave her second thoughts. She nodded and turned back toward the car.

Just as Alecksander's dissipation began, Valerie swung back around and dove into the aura as it built around him. She settled into the embrace of his arms and they emerged into the abyss together. "I told you to wait," he stated.

"And I told you I wanted to go in with you."

"Well, you're here now. Stay close."

"I've got a better idea. You look for Mordrid and I'll look for Scotty."

Alecksander wiped one of his hands across his face and sighed.

Valerie imagined his thoughts and for a quick instant wondered if she should've listened to him. He only said, "Be careful," before he vanished.

Her search went for naught. She found herself back at the car with her first step. She fisted her hands and screamed, "Alecksander!"

★★★★

Alecksander didn't warn Mordrid of his entrance into the wizard's lair. He didn't need to. The Evil Wizard knew of his approach just as he'd known of Valerie's into his office.

"Alecksander! We've awaited you," the Evil Wizard sneered as the Master Magician appeared.

"We?" Alecksander questioned, even though he already knew who the wizard had with him.

Scotty struggled, punched and kicked at the Wizard when he saw Alecksander's approach. The wizard cackled as he strengthened the firm aura of containment he held the little boy trapped in. The boy's blows didn't come close to him.

"Obeisance!" he thundered to the child.

Scotty's movements ceased. His face reddened. The boy's expression mirrored all his horrors and struggles.

Alecksander held his supernatural staff aloft. Sparkling star fragments cast out from it. "Unhand that boy!" he commanded.

"Who are you, a mere supernatural magician, to command me, the purveyor of all that is Evil?" Mordrid snarled. The awesome power of his maniacal voice echoed throughout the room he held both the boy and Alecksander entrapped in. The walls quaked.

Chapter Fifty-Six

Alecksander stared the necromancer down. He didn't pause for a breath before he responded with all the power, and maybe even a little more, of the evil he faced.

"I've become more powerful than you since last we met," he thundered. "This will be the final time you abuse the boy!"

The luminescence of his staff spread and encompassed the Master Magician. Its righteous fury illuminated him.

Rage reddened the wizard's once green eyes. A dark cloud surrounded him and his little victim. And then he vanished. The boy disappeared with him.

Alecksander followed as he too, vanished. The world he soon found himself in was like none other he'd ever known. He stared into the abyss he found himself in.

Screams, as if from unrepentant souls, tormented his ears. He sensed the essences of the ones who wailed surrounded him, but couldn't see them.

The opaqueness engulfed Alecksander. He visually searched through it until he caught a tiny pin-prick of light, which

shown out through it to him. He knew it
radiated out to him from Scotty's
blameless being.

Alecksander ran without sight toward
the light, until he came close enough to
be able to see both the Wizard and Scotty.
The shadows in the darkness he passed
through to get to Scotty wrapped themselves
around him and slowed him immeasurably.

Alecksander saw the dark ones gathered
all about Scotty. He called on his wand
of righteousness and sliced through those
around him to aid his efforts in reaching
out to the boy. But he couldn't be rid of
them.

"You're alone here in all your
valiant efforts," the voices echoed to
him. "The boy is ours." Alecksander saw
they threaded their evil ways into and
through Scotty's motionless body.

"He's an innocent!" Alecksander
declared. "Let me make a compact with
you!" At the sudden silence of those in
the damnable darkness, Alecksander took it
they listened and so he made his proposal.

"Let me impose my supernatural prowess
on the powers of the semi-dark soul of
Mordrid. He's not yet completely one of
you, but dwells between the two worlds."
Alecksander listened. The evil world
around him remained silent.

"If he wins, you get the boy. But if
I win, you get Mordrid for all eternity!"

Mordrid's evil laughter cracked the
silence. "You'll never better me down here
with all my likenesses. Above, I was the
one alone, but down here, you're the one
who's alone!

"Of course they'd rather have an

untarnished soul to impregnate with all
their evil, than one such as me who is free
to traverse both worlds and deliver
untarnished souls to them!"

He has a point. But Alecksander
noted the concerned sound in Mordrid's
voice. *Nevertheless; he's worried.* He
knew Mordrid witnessed his increased
powers.

The dimensions in the netherworld
trembled with bodiless words from the
darkness of the realm, "Let the battle
begin!"

Alecksander brandished his magical
cane in Mordrid's face. Its gold tip
sizzled.

Mordrid slithered aside from the
shadows he held Scotty captive in, and
wielded a scorpion-like dagger. It twisted
and writhed in his grip.

*I've never before seen a weapon such
as the darkness provides for Mordrid to
wield.* But it bothered the Master
Magician not.

The physical bodies of their
brandishers became non-existent as the two
weapons assumed lives of their own and met
in an aura of violence. They became a part
of their opaque surroundings.

Fire flew and shining's shattered into
the ever-existing night of the nether
world. The beings in the darkness cowered
away from the majestic magic that invaded
their world.

Night became day and day turned to
night as the weapons lightened and
darkened. The battle between the two
continued without break. It seemed there
would be no end to their conflict.

The fight between the two ended as fast as it began. Night became day, and Scotty stood at Alecksander's side as the Master Magician stood victorious over the fallen being of Mordrid.

Before their eyes the Wizard's withering essence wailed as it seeped into the darkness, which waited on the other side of the light. Alecksander and Scotty soon found themselves outside, nearby where Valerie wept on her knees.

"Valerie," the master magician soothed.

Déjà vu again set in with her when she heard his voice. *I've been in this same situation before.* She raised her attention to him without a word. Her breath whipped in when she saw both of them. *They're both here.* "You're both here!"

Valerie jumped up, ran to them, and threw her arms around both. They returned her embrace as she spoke. "I'm so happy you've come back to me!"

"I'm happy you're here, Valerie!" Scotty joyfully announced.

Alecksander's embrace tightened around each of them.

"I looked for you, but I couldn't find you. I'm so sorry I couldn't help you," Valerie cried to the little boy.

"It's okay. I told you I'm almost a man. Me and Alecksander took care of that mean old wizard."

"He's gone. You're still a healer," Alecksander acknowledged. His hands found hers.

At his touch; Valerie knew of the heartbreak of their previous lifetimes.

Her heart rose with the eternal happiness she knew would now be theirs. "Yes. I believe in magic," she breathed in belated answer to his original question.

A little hand landed on their joined hands. "Me, too!" Scotty squealed.

They both gazed down on the little boy they knew always would be theirs.

"Can I call you 'Mommy'?"

The tug on Valerie's heartstrings brought tears to her eyes. She remembered his words about mommys.

"And you're my *Daddy*?"

Alecksander reached down and rustled the hair on Scotty's head. "Yes, I'd love to be, son."

Epilogue

"Do you, Valerie Baldwin, take Alecksander Stone to love and cherish for the rest of your life?"

Valerie's heart rose as she dove into the depths of Alexander's mischievous brown eyes. They appeared especially playful to her today. She broke her attention long enough to look down to their ring bearer.

The happiness on Scotty's little face melted her heart. Her fingers trembled as she slid the ring onto Alecksander's finger. "I do." *I've never known such love.*

"And do you, Alecksander Stone, take Valerie Baldwin as the woman you will keep by your side to love and to cherish forever?"

Scotty beamed up at him when he retrieved his ring from the boy's pillow.

"Yes, Forever."

Valerie thrilled at the connotation behind his answer. *I'm so glad we've finally connected with each other.*

Alecksander embraced Valerie and kissed her. He kissed her with a passion

only a man who'd searched forever for his
love could give.

THE END

Thank you for taking time to read
Informed. If you enjoyed it, please
consider telling your friends or posting a
short review. Word of mouth is an author's
best friend and much appreciated.

To know when my next books are available,
be sure to sign up for my newsletter at
www.authorjanetteharjo.blogspot.com. You
can also follow me on Twitter
@JanetteHarjo, or like my Facebook page at
https://www.facebook.com/janette.harjo?fre
f=tsPage/137667526246086

Property of
Grace Baptist Church

Made in the USA
Charleston, SC
01 May 2015